THE

SHIRE

Walter E. Ledwith

La Maison Publishing, Inc.
Vero Beach, Florida
The Hibiscus City
lamaisonpublishing@gmail.com

Dedication

Thanks to Everyone I've Ever Met

Contents

THE SHIRE

When my friends call from New York, and I tell them I am living in a trailer park in Florida, they imagine me in a rundown single-wide with neighbors that have bears chained in the front yard, whiskey breath, wearing yesterday's clothes. Of course, my cracker neighbors consume copious amounts of alcohol and are copulating around the clock, stopping only to eat, sleep, and defecate. It is presumed the children of these folks are low-functioning victims of alcohol fetal syndrome, parented by people who themselves need parenting. Seeing it as an opportunity to watch a full-blown stereo-type in action, I play along.

"The world sure is different when you're looking at it from the heart of a trailer park," I'd tell them.

"You poor dear. . . are you afraid going home at night?"

"I don't go out after dark."

Beverly tried to comfort me, telling me it was only temporary and that *"we're going to get you through this."* She had a rather dim view of the world, and I think it came from her job as a forensic medical examiner for the City of NY. When not with her cadavers, she was on the 32nd floor of a high-rise on third avenue. Sitting with her cats, she'd watch the lighted ribbons below and the traffic's constant flow.

"Do you need anything? I can send some dishes . . . and I have an extra set of pots."

"No, I have all that—furniture too. It's like staying in a rental, actually. The people I bought the house from left me with all that I needed to get started. Nice folks."

Beverly wasn't being mean in her attitude towards Florida's less sophisticated residents. All she knew was what she saw on her monitors and phone. I was guilty of the same prejudice. When my kids were young and losing interest in their school work, I would admonish them and try to instill in them a fear of living in a box set on cinder-blocks, with broken steps, flanked by grease-covered barbeque grills. I painted a pretty scary picture of what it's like to be poor and that it was not an option.

"You'd better learn how to do something in this world, or you'll be standing in line waiting for handouts," which worked pretty good until the last year of high school. By then, my tales of the 'great depression' drew chuckles and snide remarks. My son has always been adept at facetious sarcasm. When I told him of my move to Florida, he asked me,

"Gee dad, is living in a trailer like what you told us when we were kids?" In my mind's eye, I could see the snarky smile on his face, which I returned 'tout suite.'

"Well. . . it's not like any place else I've ever lived before; I can tell you that."

Alexey and I both enjoyed a verbal joust, and he was really good at it, something I was proud of. A chip off the old block, so to speak. But behind the banter, there was genuine concern, "Don't worry, Dad, we'll get you out of there." But he just couldn't resist, "If you work hard and study, you won't ever have to live in a trailer again."

****

Malcolm is a filmmaker friend of mine living in Manhattan. High above the busy sidewalk, he watches humanity schooling along the canyons of the city. It fascinates him, my living in a trailer park, and he wants complete details about the people and the goings on in the community. He's the kind of guy who rides the subway, so to be with the 'real people'. He'll get on the 'A' train and ride it to the end of the line. Then back again. Back and forth from 207th street to Far Rockaway until he has had his fill of the masses. He likes to visit the bodegas in the Bronx, and while using the botanical gardens or little Italy as an excuse for travel, his true destination was the different shops in the area where he would hang out and play dominoes. Sometimes winning! The aromas, the ethnicity, and the society of people drew him back again and again. He said the atmosphere was intoxicating. I've always thought the aromas in the bodegas were from the over-ripe plantains and the yellowing chicken legs in the display case. A sure way to lose your appetite if you're trying to diet.

But I, too, respect these good folks. The pictures displayed behind the counter showed their home and the work it took to move to the U.S. and open a business. Industrious and brave, they carved for themselves a niche in a great metropolis, and they were proud people.

"This place is not quite like you imagine, Malcolm. Perhaps what you're looking for is true somewhere, but not here."

I told him we had two large lakes in the trailer park, well stocked with fish. Folks jump in their golf carts in the morning, drive to their favorite fishing spot, and start the day competing with the Osprey for the bass. Beginning at daybreak, cyclists circle the park, greeting friends and neighbors on their power walks. Anglers, cyclists, and walkers wave and bid each other good morning. The rabbits and squirrels chase each other about with abandon, without fear. The Sandhill cranes that walk along the shore stand five feet tall. A verity of ducks stroll with the wood-stork and the ubiquitous Ibis's, avoiding the fast-moving squirrels as they forage. A large turtle warms himself on the pavement, collecting the energy to begin his day. Otters crawl and play on a log in the middle of the lake.

"And my favorite . . . is the Anhinga. This guy does his fishing underwater, and when he comes up for air, he looks like a miniature Loch Ness monster patrolling the lake. After swimming and filling his belly, he faces the sun, spreads his wings, and dries himself majestically, stating his 'I AM.'"

"Not exactly what I was hoping for!" complained Malcolm

"Well, wait, there's more. There is a large clubhouse here with a billiard room and a library. A café, work-out room, and event hall, complete with a stage for shows. Outside, there is a full-size heated pool for use the year around. Bocce courts, shuffleboard, tennis courts—"

"You're boring meeee . . . what happened to the drunken orgies, the wife swapping, and craziness? Tell me about someone hiding from the mob with pit bulls for pillows."

"So far, I've met retired military, teachers, small business owners, and such. Seems most people are living off their 401Ks, pensions, social security and have enough disposable income to indulge themselves with retirement toys. It's the quietest place I've ever lived, as well. It's an age-restricted community, fifty-five and older, so you're not getting the thump-thump of car radios at three in the morning. Lots of gray hairs but little noise."

I didn't like disappointing Malcolm, even felt bad for letting him down. But then I realized that although the ambiance of Seaside was shire-like, the population, myself included, were all fucking weird. I don't know if it's the place that makes us that way or that everybody has always been weird, and I didn't bother to notice. The fact of the matter is that this is a fishbowl with a cavalcade of characters.

"Hold on man, just hold on. There's more. We have it all here. Tattooed ladies galore. And I'm not talking about a rose discreetly placed on a shoulder. I'm talking tattoos that cover an entire arm or leg; sometimes with cryptic messages known only to the bearer — tattoos that have faded and changed with the landscape of its canvass. We have handicapped people who ride motorcycles and scooters. For sure, there is a fair share of folks from the witness protection program or those released from the hospital with medication, which we hope they're taking. I've heard stories about bordellos and pot growers, even murder, though the murder people snuck in from outside to do a drug deal. Everyone is from somewhere else. Every accent in the country is spoken here, some of which I don't understand."

"Ah . . . a Tower of Babel . . . that could be interesting."

"And a good number of them ride three-wheeled bicycles. What does that tell you?"

"That the residents of your Shire ride around in chariots babbling incoherently?"

"Exactly!"

"But couldn't you scrounge up a meth lab somewhere in the trailer park?"

Malcolm had modest success years back with short films and a documentary on flesh-eating bacteria. He was always looking for new material and had a cadre of friends who he badgered for stories. I wouldn't be able to help him this time though. Yes, these people were covered in tattoos. They talked funny, drove yellow Mustang convertibles, and pushed their dogs around in baby carriages, but they were also the people who worked at the food banks. The folks who tutor kids in reading and math, who visit the elderly in their homes and in the hospital. These people are the salt of the earth, the ones who actually do something to make the world a better place. Not at all like our group in New York, whose expertise lies in complaining about life's inconveniences.

"I don't think there's anything here for you right now, Malcolm. But hey, I just got to Florida. Let's see how it works out. I'll let you know if I come across anything interesting."

After hanging up the phone, I realized it would make an interesting project to collect sketches of my neighbors and the goings on in the park. Vignettes of our microcosm. It would take my mind off the lawyers and my divorce. We certainly are an eclectic group, and it would keep me busy. I may very well have my own little *'Tortilla Flat'* going on and should take advantage of it while I drift through the never-never land of the legal system. I would start with the cul-de-sac on which I lived. Using the hood of my Jeep as a desk, I would document all that I see. Opening my laptop, I started a new Word document, calling it 'Thumbnails.' I entered the first name on my list.

SEÑOR SANCHEZ AND MARIPOSA

Senor Sanchez is in his late seventies. Bald, short, and stocky, five foot six or so. He is a tightly wound man in search of a trigger. He is of Puerto Rican decent from New York City's Washington Heights. I lived in the same neighborhood when I was a boy and was taken by the coincidence. After all the years and the many miles traveled, we both have come to the same place. He lives across the street, and once again, he is my neighbor. Almost at the beginning of our conversation, he brought up the murder of the young Mickey Farmer at High-Bridge Park pool in the late fifties. It was a big thing at the time. He retold the story with vivid detail as though it took place only yesterday. Mickey Farmer was a wheelchair-bound twelve-year-old who was brought to the balcony of the pool to sun himself and watch the children swim. I had not known Mickey personally, but the consensus of opinion at the time was that he was an extremely unpleasant fellow who cursed profusely while insulting people. I think nowadays we might call it Tourette's syndrome. Everyone was fair game for him, and he acted with impunity. He invoked sorrow and pity from people, and he knew it; that gave him license. His luck ran out when, one day, he cursed out the wrong person. A young Puerto Rican kid became enraged by the verbal assault and, driven by machismo, took out his switch blade and stabbed young Farmer, killing him. The musical 'Westside Story' was a very real situation on the West side of Manhattan at this time, and this event, of course, inflamed tensions. Senor Sanchez remembers the tensions the newly immigrated emigrants from Puerto Rico felt. I can see he still feels very angry. But if it were not this, it would be something else. Senor Sanchez is a walking, talking, text book case of OCD. After the landscapers cut the grass, he follows up with his lawn mover to make sure all the grass is even and at the same height. He is the first one to place his trash out a full day before pick-up. His house and his plantings are meticulously kept. He sweeps the sidewalk and gutters in the street once a week. He has a chihuahua, what used to be called 'tea cup dog,' that he walks around the house a dozen or so times a day. Around and round, past the ducks, the lake, the palms, and the pines. Round and round the house, again and again.

Senor Sanchez is a helicopter parent, on task, always.

"Why are you going that way?" he would ask Chichi, no matter which direction chichi might have chosen. "What are you afraid of . . . there's nobody there!" Chichi ignored him, going as far as her leach would allow. Sniffing everything in sight. She would bark fearlessly at passersby, and you would think she was the size of a lion by her body language,

"Yip......yip …..yip….." she roars, in barely audible, terrifying tones as she lunges forward.

Of course, Senor Sanchez, as trainer, is quick to jump in with commands. You would think he was training a pit bull. Not a problem, though. Chichi knows she is loved and that this behavior was an expression of that love. You can feel the oxytocin flowing.

Mariposa is rarely seen outside of her house. She is about five-foot-two, stocky, with a bushy hair style. Sometimes, she would walk the property examining the work that's been done and approve or make recommendations as to what should change. Standing together, they complement each other perfectly, portraying an American gothic ala San Juan PR. She is the glue that holds their life together. They have worked hard, saved their money and now live comfortably in a world so safe and secure they can spend their time quibbling over the most insignificant details, creating monsters and enemies from what is most readily at hand. There is no doubt that she is in charge. She orders Senor Sanchez around and he passes it on to Chichi. So what's wrong with that if it works so well?

At present there is a little war going on between Senor Sanchez and his neighbor who lives catty-corner to his house. In the center of the cul-de-sac, there is a blue bag of dog shit lying on the road that no one has claimed responsibility for. This morning, Senor Sanchez came to see me as I hosed down my truck.

"This guy thinks that it's my dogs' shit when it ain't. I always use green bags instead of blue. Everybody knows that. Next time, I'm gonna give him a piece of my mind."

"What did he say?"

"Nothing . . . he waived, and I could tell his wave meant it was my fault. I thought he was a nice guy . . . I'm gonna show him!"

"Can you read his mind?" I asked, "how do you know?"

"That kind is all alike."
So, this is what geriatric warfare looks like.

ALABAMA

I like to work outside, so I've set myself up using the trunk of my jeep as a standing desk. Nicely tucked under my car-port, out of the sun, I do a lot of stuff on my truck desk — from coffee and cake in the morning to writing in my journal in the twilight. Bills are paid, and I keep my correspondence up to date. I also get to see a lot of what's going on in the neighborhood. I have become a regular feature, and folks expect I will be there when they pass by. It's part of the routine.

Alabama passes by several times a day on the way to the dog park down the street.

She is a tall woman… bushy hair, late fifties, maybe, with tattoos covering her legs from her ankles to her thighs. She speaks with a thick southern accent and is always willing to share her opinions whether they are asked for or not.

"My name is Alice, but everybody calls me Alabama 'cause that's where I come from."

Her dogs barked a lot, especially at other walkers and their dogs, big or small. She lets out a warning, "Jack Russell, Jack Russell," explaining their behavior as she reins in her beast.

"Why did you give both of your dogs the same name?" I asked her while working in the garden.

"That ain't their names! Don't you know nothin' 'bout dogs? That's the kind of dog they are. They're an aggressive breed. Their names are Heckle and Jeckle."

"They both look alike. How do you tell them apart?"

"One of 'dem is male, can't ya see?"

"I didn't look."

"Don't know how yah missed dem, Heckle's got a big pair."

She loves to talk about herself. At our first meeting, I found out she was studying to be a medical transcriptionist, where she lived, how long she lived there, and what she paid for her house. The why for the move was most interesting.

"My husband tried to kill me, so I set him up so the police could bust 'em, and then I got out of town. He's a real bastard and will do anything for a buck. He's done two years so far, got five more to go."

"Do you think he'll come looking for you?"

"I know he will. But I got the perfect murder planned, forensics and all, so I'll be ready for him when he gets out."

"They're awfully good at finding evidence these days, Alabama. Best not to get involved in that kind of stuff."

"I know. I watch all the CSI shows on TV. That's how I know how to plan the perfect murder."

"Well, I hope you never have to do that."

"Easy for you to say, but I gotta' do what I gotta' do."

She cleans houses, cares for the elderly, is a pet sitter, and more. Alabama doesn't own a car. She drives a red electric scouter. She didn't venture out of the park very often, so the scooter worked for all her needs.

"Saves me on gas, insurance, registration, and all the rest. I don't go nowhere anyways, so it works fine for me."

I've seen her on the road into town, riding in the bike lane. Between the scooters, bicycles, three-wheelers, and motorized wheelchairs, it gets pretty busy in that lane. And they move along at a brisk pace. She says sometimes they race. Whenever I see her on her red scooter, I think about her and her cohorts racing along Rt.60 in a scene from Stanley Kramer's 'It's a mad, mad, mad, mad world' with their helmets and American flags waving, racing along in a fury making a surreal dimensional shift in space and time.

We stopped talking after a disagreement over drugs. She decided she would supplement her income by selling pot to her neighbors in the community. I must have seemed like a likely candidate, so she made her pitch.

"It's so good, half a joint will last yah all day."

"That's not for me. I'd never get anything done. It's the last thing I need. I know people who spend years on their couch from smoking that stuff. And at two hundred dollars an ounce, I don't see how you can afford it."

"It's two eighty and ounce! . . . I always make at least a hundred for one of my jobs, so afta' a couple of them, I can pay for it."

Her pot guy, as she called him, was part of the landscaping crew in the shire. A bearded Jamaican gentleman who wore a skeleton mask as he zipped around on his machine at a frenzied pace. She sounded quite taken with him, so I suspect they were involved in other ways as well. I'd see her blowing kisses at him as he roared by on his machine. The landscaping company lost their contract at Seaside, so I haven't seen him around lately. I don't know if business continued because we stopped talking after her sales pitch. I think Alabama, or her bearded skeleton, thought I might be a liability and decided to steer clear. I got the cold shoulder whenever she walked by. If she was with a friend, there was a frozen silence as they passed. Over time, things became more cordial, and we exchanged niceties. Not seeing her in a while, I asked some passing dog walkers how she was doing. Evidently, she had moved to Ft. Lauderdale to be with her daughter after she landed a big job in real estate.

"She's taking care of the house and the grandson while the daughter works," the man said skeptically, his companion shaking her head. "I've met the daughter. I don't think so."

I hope Alabama is doing well. She's a smart and resourceful woman. Just someone who can't find her way off the rollercoaster. She can't read the exit signs.

PASSERSBY 1

A gentleman riding a three-wheeled cycle traces the perimeter of the cul-de-sac. He is listening to a handheld transistor radio, wearing an old tee-shirt with advertising that dates to the sixties. From its small speaker, I can hear music that sounds like a Good Humor truck back when I was a kid. I have a Pavlovian response of excited anticipation upon hearing that glorious music played. Only happiness can come from a Good Humor truck. Parents, children, everyone was always glad to see the ice cream man. He would arrive every day after school, bringing order to the world. The job didn't pay much, but there was a lot of love.

New to the cavalcade, this gentleman has passed by several times, and each time, I revel in the joyous sounds. Today, he could use a shower and a shave. I wonder if the gentleman is aware of the effect he is producing with his blast from the past. Maybe this is a sinister bit of guerilla theater. He, knowing the effect the music has, leaves a trail of frustration and disappointment in his wake. Is that why he's smiling? Is this payback for all the times he didn't have the money for a good humor bar? Is he exacting revenge upon the world?

Or maybe he's just an old guy following his doctor's orders to *get some exercise.* The wife nags him until he gives in. He hates being told what to do and resents the fact she is right, but the music takes his mind off it all. I'll never know unless I ask, which I don't think I'll do. I prefer the mystery.

ARCHIE AND COMPANY

Archie just appeared. The folks next door moved out in the middle of the night, and the next morning, Archie was moving in. Bob and Alice left everything behind and hightailed it back to Missouri. Alice was beginning to fall more often, and a move to be close to family was in order.

My new neighbor had help with his move from his 'cousins.' They made short work of it, replacing toilets, repairing the AC and generally setting it up so Archie could move around freely, unaided, with easy access to his car. They did a thorough job, and he got around pretty good. Archie's upper torso bends at a forty-five-degree angle to his center of gravity, making him look top-heavy and about to fall over. He moves about like a daddy-longlegs spider, from chair to table to sofa, in a choreographed routine. He lives alone and manages quite well.

Archie kept the doctors busy. Several times a week, I would see him early in the morning, driving off to some appointment. He would wave as he drove by.

He told me he had owned and operated a car care center in Hartford, Connecticut, before moving to Florida and I sensed it was a very successful business. *So why is he living here?*

A rich miser? His cousins confirmed this as they talked freely about who would inherit what. They are reminiscent of Tolkien characters, with Archie being the master of the gold, aided by his cohorts. One cousin, close in age, dwarf-like, had long gray hair with a full, pointed beard to match. He grunted a lot and talked to himself while going about his business. His brother was Elfin-like, thin and wiry. Back when Archie was erect, he must have stood a full head above his minions. The Elf did the physical work, the power washing and such. He believed that a revolution was necessary in the country in order to bring it back to the days of Regan. The dwarf took out the trash and ran errands, stopping by daily to check on things. He told a story about how they were chased from their community in Sebastian. Never did say what the issue was. They all sold their houses and moved to Vero Beach, in different parks, but close by. *What the hell could these characters have done to be run out of a trailer park in Sebastian?* For the most part they avoided talking with people, keeping their business close to the vest and within the family. I was the exception. When introducing myself to my new neighbor, I commented on his name, saying that one of my favorite movies was 'The last time I saw Archie' with Robert Mitchum. It's about a guy who, after being drafted into the Army, decides to make the best of it and turn a profit. After success with all his scheming, he's asked how he pulled it off. He replied, "With a clipboard. People see a clipboard as having authority. Like when seeing a stethoscope around someone's neck, you see a doctor. In the logistics world, a clipboard is a symbol of power." Archie remembered the movie, and Robert Mitchum was one of his favorite actors.

"I haven't heard that name in years," he declared and I was in like Flynn because how could anybody who liked Robert

Mitchum be all that bad. Over time, I began to get a picture of Archie and his crew. Something about them reminded me of 'Vinnie the Chin'[1] down in New York's Greenwich Village. Part of me believed that all the drama around Archie's infirmities was a cover for his illegal business operations. Far-fetched, but I wanted to believe it.

Archie was a horndog. He had been married four times and had two children. The ex-wives all lived back in Connecticut. The kids, grown, moved to opposite ends of the country. The son to Fairbanks, Alaska, and the daughter to St. John's Bayou in southern Louisiana. Eddie, the dwarf, said Archie was trying to get the ex-wives to move down to Florida to live with him. Any one of them or all of them.

"So far, two of them said they'd think about it."

"That's a lot of women to pleasure. Would that be good for him? You know, at his age and all," I asked, trying not to laugh. We both leaned on the hood of my truck as he filled me in on the goings-on.

"He's going to get a penile implant and swears that after that, he can handle all comers." Eddie appeared to believe him. "The nurses at the clinic love him and shower him with attention. The concierge and the parking lot attendants run to greet him when we pull up for his appointment."

"They have valet parking at the implant clinic?"

"Oh yeah. There's coffee, donuts, and cable TV in the waiting room. They even change the station to his favorite news program when he comes in," he said, laughing. "I told them CNN might give him a heart attack."

"So, servicing four women is okay, but the wrong cable news program might kill him?"

---

[1] 'Vinnie the chin': Head of the Gambino crime family.

"I was just having a little fun. Me and Archie laughed all the way home. The nurses just love the guy and want to make him happy. They all tell him they wish their husbands were more like him."

"That's some story."

"It's all true. Everything is scheduled, but first, he's going to have surgery on his shoulder." In the weeks that followed, the house was painted, and new shrubs were planted in the front of the house.

Eddie was a character himself. He spoke of himself and described his life in the third person, as though he were telling a story. At one time or other, he ran an answering service, a messenger service and a strip club in Hartford. Claims he did very well for himself in all three enterprises. He owned a large house that housed a trophy wife and her two daughters. The wife didn't like him running a strip club, and they divorced. She got the house, but he continued to live there, building an apartment in the rear and carrying on as before. The daughters loved him and are close to him to this day. The strip joint was his favorite. He was a father-figure, confidant, and mentor to the girls working at the club and made a lot of money doing it. He must have spent it all cause now he lives in a modest apartment and drives an old Chevrolet that is in need of some work.

Gil, the Elfin cousin, was not as talkative, but over time, I was able to piece together a history. He drove a diesel pick-up truck and carried a swath of keys that jingled on his belt. He and his wife did handyman jobs for neighbors to keep busy. He was rather vocal though, when it came to politics. He was a steadfast Trump supporter and had a deep mistrust of the government and its liberal policies.

"Their kids are killing each other wholesale. They don't know if they are a boy or a girl or which bathroom to use, and it doesn't ever occur to these people that maybe it's the way they think that's the problem'. Nooo . . . they'd rather blame inanimate objects or Donald Trump!" His wife stood beside him, nodding her approval. She was a big woman, a few inches taller than Gil and was smitten with her man and his views of the world. They were a couple you wouldn't take notice of in Walmart. He told me he owned a pool company back in Connecticut and had been wintering in Florida for decades. "We're gonna pack it in and move down here next year. Can't afford to live there anymore with the taxes and all."

The surgery that was supposed to restore the use of Archies right arm did not go well. There were complications from the beginning, accompanied by a lingering infection. With a 101* fever, Eddie drove Archie to the hospital for tests and blood work. As required, he was also tested for COVID-19, which came back positive. They quarantined Archie in the COVID-19 isolation ward, and the case changed from complications after surgery to a COVID-19 case. Two days later, Archie passed from this world. His fever rose, and he expired.

Gil, his wife and Eddie took mementos and a few small appliances to their cars and placed the rest of Archies belongings on the lawn for waste management to pick up. The kids wanted nothing to do with any of it. The familiars of Archies life were at the curb for all to see and misconstrue their relevance. A nihilistic existential metaphor laid out on the lawn. A grim reminder for all those who are held captive by physicality.

The last time I saw Archie he was watering the plants on his screen porch, talking to his cat.

THE JAZZ FUNERAL

There is a gentleman living in the shire, who every day, morning and evening, walked his dog throughout the trailer park. His name is Alfred. Steadying himself on his canvas perambulator, the dog on the leash pulled him along the road. He rode his fold-up chariot as though it were a motorcycle. The dog pranced ahead, as proud as a husky leading his team. Together, they left a trail of oxytocin in their wake, rain or shine, true to their daily routine.

Maxwell, of the Shih Tzu breed, had lived his entire life in the shire. He was a gift given by a concerned brother who worried that his now languid sibling would be lonely and needed a companion. From the very beginning, their relationship was a beautiful symbiosis, rich in mutual benefits. They were best friends right out of the gate. Both felt incomplete when not together. They established a routine which became a vital part of their life-force. They lived their life to the fullest, unaware of the turmoil in the world and despite any infirmities they might personally have. They liked — unless given reason not to, all the people they met daily on their constitutional. Alfred would stop the carriage, and they would hold court for a short time before moving on to the next person. A sort of mobile receiving line. Life was good, and Alfred and Maxwell reminded everyone of that. They didn't seem to know what a bad day was.

Alfred, after recovering from several surgical procedures addressing bone loss, sold his big house in the city and moved to the Shire. He planned to take advantage of its amenities while continuing with his rehabilitation. The Shire is nestled in a small town that has all the infrastructure and services needed to cater to the care and comfort of senior citizens. With Maxwell's help, Alfred made a speedy, robust recovery. Their itinerary was full. Between their walks, swimming mid-afternoon, and their daily business routine, they were always busy. Alfred was an excellent cook and took the time to prepare tasty meals, much to the delight of neighbors who *just 'happened'* to stop by around dinnertime. Maxwell only ate top-of-the-line dog food shipped from all over the world. He had a discerning palate with a preference for the Wild Rabbit and Pacific Salmon. The images on the television upset Maxwell, so they didn't watch TV. Instead, they played with toys, or Alfred would play Bach on his piano, mesmerizing the little wolf. Maxwell liked all kinds of music, but his favorite tune was 'You ain't nothin' but a hound dog' by Elvis Presley. He would croon along with Alfred in a howling duet, energizing them both for their evening walk. On Sunday mornings, they would leave early for the beach before the crowds arrived and had the ocean to themselves. They walked along the shore and Maxwell played tag with the surf. They lived this way for years, enjoying the *salt life*.

****

Maxwell had not been feeling well, and it was oblivious. On some days, one had to look hard to find the usual exuberance that was core to his character. After a while, he would return to his old self, and they would continue with their routine — for a period of time. The intervals of lethargy became more frequent. More and more often, he took in the world from the comfort of his carriage. During those times, he sat expressionless and stoically accepted the good wishes of the people they met, all calling for his speedy recovery. It began with his tiring on the way home, and soon after, he only pulled his chariot halfway around the lake. The veterinarian said he didn't know what was wrong with him. He could only guess and needed further tests. Albert wanted nothing to do with guessing.

"Well, then just make him comfortable and make sure he eats. Once he loses his appetite, it's all downhill. I am going to proscribe some minerals and vitamins to boost his immune system. I hope it helps. The best of luck, Mr. Katz."

Maxwell was a fighter and held on, doing the best he could for several months. There were good days, and there were bad days. More and more often, Alfred would cut short their walks so as not to exhaust Maxwell. In dog years, they were both the same age, and Alfred was happy to accommodate his Shih Tzu. On one such evening, they agreed to a short walk, and after circling the cul-de-sac a couple of times, they returned home to rest and settle in for the night.

But Maxwell didn't want to go to his bed. He jumped in Alfred's lap, and they rocked quietly with soft words and healing strokes. Maxwell jumped up and put his paws over Alfred's shoulders, licking his ear and whimpering. He needed

Alfred's body heat, and Alfred understood. They rocked together until they fell asleep.

Alfred awoke in the middle of the night and realized the whimpering had stopped. His friend was cold, stiff, and wasn't breathing. *Maxwell est mort.* Unsure of what to feel, he hugged him and closed his eyes. Tears rolled down his cheeks as he drifted off into a sleepy reverie.

****

Beyond the windows, the sun rose in the distance, signaling the day was to begin. Alfred awoke, grappling with the notion that Maxwell would not be licking his face that morning or any other. No longer would he have a companion who followed him everywhere and kept him on track. *I won't have to scold him for running around the living room anymore.*

He faced the loss and struggled to believe it was so. Until he could sort it out, he decided to maintain the schedule they normally kept and take a last walk together. With Maxwell draped over his shoulder, he took the fold-up carriage from the carport and set it up alongside the road. He tried to make the dead dog comfortable, but being stiff as a board made it difficult. Maxwell, arms stretched out, eyes fixed with a frozen stare, looked straight ahead like a sculpture in situ. Mrs. Sanchez lived across the street and was walking her dog with her husband when she saw what was going on. She understood immediately.

"Pablo, here, take the leash. The old man's dog is dead."

Mrs. Sánchez crossed the street to console him.

"Alfred, I am so sorry for your loss. We loved Maxwell and will miss him a lot. Can I help you with anything?"

"Thank you, Mariposa. I think we're good. We're going for one last walk. He'd have liked that. Then, I'll bury him behind the house. He used to play with the squirrels back there, and he would have liked that, too. After that, I guess it's just a matter of me getting used to him not being around."

"Can I come along, Alfred? You know, . . . out of respect for Maxwell."

"That would be nice. Thank you, Mariposa."

Ed Holmes and Roy Wilson went together to offer their condolences with kind words and genuine sympathy.

"We're right next door should you need us," Ed assured him, and Roy concurred,

"Anytime, Alfred, we're always here for you."

Alfred adjusted the seat belt on the carriage, as Mariposa explained.

"He's taking the dog for one last walk. Kinda' beautiful, ya know. I'm going along to make it like a funeral procession, like back home in Puerto Rico."

"Yes, yes, the last ride through the old neighborhood. Excellent idea, I'm in." Roy said, falling behind Mariposa. Ed Holmes joined him, "Me too . . . I really liked the little guy!"

Alfred started slowly, his leg stiff from sleeping in the chair all night. He threw his leg out, anchored it, and pushed the carriage forward. The procession had begun with the bereaved in the lead, Mariposa behind, and Ed and Roy following along.

Just ahead, Mrs. Canady was watering her flower beds. She saw the procession coming down the road and understood what was happening. Dropping the hose, she put on her pandemic mask and joined the group of mourners. She had her smart phone with her and decided to share.

"Hello, Edna, it's Anne. Guess where I am? I'm in a funeral procession on Sandpiper drive. Yup . . . you know Alfred, the guy who cooks and has a Chinese dog? . . . Ya, well, the dog died, and they're having a funeral procession for him. I liked him too. Sure . . . sure, come on down."

"Tell her to bring an umbrella!" Roy said, taking his cell phone from his pocket.

Anne nodded. "And Edna, bring an umbrella."

Roy Wilson called home to speak with his wife.

"Hi Cheryl, . . . listen, Ya know that recording you have on your iPod of that jazz funeral we saw in New Orleans? Yup, that one. Well, Alfred's dog died last night, and we are having a funeral procession for him. Yup, we can make it like a big easy funeral. . . . I thought so too. We're only a block away. Could you bring that down here? Great, . . . oh yah, bring the umbrellas too. Thanks, babe. See you in a bit."

She arrived soon after, passed out the umbrellas, and turned on her iPod.

"Now we have a funeral!" laughed Roy, seeing the people swaying and the umbrellas twirling. Up ahead, a masked Mrs. Lowell stood beside a road sign with bold letters:

'Wear a double mask'

With a raised fist, she yelled at the group from across the street.

"You're going to kill us all! This is unacceptable. I am going to call the authorities!"

"What's she talking about?" asked Ed. "We're fifty feet away from her."

"They're truly frightened is all," Mariposa said, twirling her umbrella. They're not being themselves. Everybody's got to do what they feel is right. Arguing with them doesn't help. Ignore them like me and Alfred do."

Erik Czerny passed by on his motorcycle, his wife riding along in the sidecar. They saw what was happening and immediately understood what they had to do. They continued on to Frosty Daniel's place and told Frosty and his wife what was happening down the street. Everyone agreed they should join the parade, and so they did. Erik and Betty would take the lead of Maxwell's entourage, and Frosty and his wife would bring up the rear.

When passing Cheryl Wilson, Erik asked her if he could connect her iPod to his speakers for greater volume. When he did, the music spread throughout the entire Shire; the street became awash with the music of a New Orleans funeral. Erik moved to the front to lead the cortege. People had been joining the parade all the while, some masked, some not. Folks with parasols, walking sticks and their dogs were leaving their homes along the route and filling the ranks. The funeral procession was by then almost a block long, as people in motorized wheelchairs and golf carts followed behind those walking. Frosty Daniels capped the rear.

When they reached the Seaside clubhouse, Erik pulled into the parking lot to pause and give the folks some time to rest. There were bathrooms and cold water available, and soon, there was a line for both. Frosty Daniels pulled up alongside Erik with 'In A Godda Da Vita"[2] playing on his bike.

"Crank it up, Frosty," laughed Erik.

Alfred lifted Maxwell from the carriage, now in full rigor, placed his paws over his shoulders, and walked to the lake. "Come on buddy, we're gonna' dance."

---

[2] 'In the Garden of life' Iron Butterfly, 1968

Some of the folks in the parking lot paired off and danced. Others watched, spinning their umbrellas and keeping time to the music with their heads. Alfred danced like Fred Astaire, with abandon, remembering the countless hours they spent together at the lake exploring its shores. The sun was shining. There was music, laughter, and the company of good friends.

"We're all here for you, Max," Alfred whispered in his ear. Gratitude for all they had shared together was now a part of his bereavement. He still felt the lingering sense of loss weighing on his chest, but it was subsiding. He smiled when he thought of all the joy Maxwell brought to the people gathered. He made everyone laugh and shared his excitement for life freely and without reservation.

The rejuvenated entourage re-grouped to finish their cortege. It was not far to Alfred's house and the pace of the procession quickened with the Jazz music now being played. Along the way, people waved from their porches, enjoying the parade and its upbeat music. Others yelled about masks and super-spreaders. The happy cortege continued on its way to Maxwell's house. When they arrived, the mourners became a crowd that filled the cul-de-sac. They congregated awhile, making their goodbyes, and disappeared as stealthily as they appeared. A few stayed behind with Alfred. Roy Wilson and Ed Holmes offered to ready Maxwell's grave and dug a pit under the Holly Tree, as Alfred wished. Mrs. Candy would bring a ham, Mariposa a roast chicken, and Mrs. Levi offered her gefilte fish.

"We'll have a beautiful wake!" chimed Mrs. Canady.

They agreed to meet at seven o'clock to bury Maxwell. Then, they would share a celebratory feast in honor of their canine friend. Alfred wheeled Maxwell's carriage into the laundry room and went inside to take a nap. It had been a full day, and there was more to come that evening.

****

Alfred made brochettes and chilled the wine. His guests arrived one after another, arms laden with food. The kitchen table became a buffet of the most delectable morsels, and the company was not shy about enjoying them. They toasted Maxwell, his life, and themselves as the steadfast friends of a noble spirit. When it was time for the burial, Alfred pushed the carriage one last time to the gravesite. He lifted his little friend from the carriage, gave him a hug, and passed Maxwell on to Ed to place in the grave.

"Should we get a crate, or a box, or something to put him in?" asked Mrs. Canady.

"At least a shroud," mumbled Mrs. Levi.

"No, it's fine. He'll be able to fertilize the tree this way." Alfred said, gently shoveling dirt into the grave. "Wait, I almost forgot!" He reached into his pockets, removed the Shin Tsu's favorite toys, and tossed them into the grave. "He loved his toys."

Maxwell lay in the shallow pit, staring up at the mourners with arms raised as though he were imploring them not to leave. They passed the shovel around, and each took a turn filling Maxwell's last resting place. It didn't take long for a small mound to rise above the ground. Mariposa placed flowers on top. Mrs. Canady outlined it with seashells, and Ed Holmes set a white cross at its head. Alfred and Roy Wilson listened solemnly as Mrs. Levi recited a Kaddish, a prayer for the dead. After holding hands in a prolonged 'moment of silence,' the mourners left for the house, one behind the other. Alfred lingered behind for a few last words.

"Seems like yesterday my brother dropped you off at the house. You were a handful at first, but you turned into the smartest dog I ever met, almost telepathic. I'm gonna' miss you, and I'm grateful for everything you brought into my life. Goodbye buddy. I'll see you later. I have to attend to the living."

Alfred returned to the house to find everyone with a plate and the air buzzing with conversation.

"It's not a wake if you have no body." Talking to Mrs. Canady, Mrs. Levi was firm. "No body! . . . then it's a short Shiva."

"We're all together. That's all that matters." Mariposa said while munching on a chicken leg.

"The Mayor has gone too far this time, way over recommendations." Roy lectured Ed, explaining the fine points of the town's new budget proposal.

"More wine, anyone?" Alfred asked, making the rounds and pouring refills. "I'm sorry I don't have any Manischewitz, Mrs. Levi, but it all happened so quick and —"

"Not to worry," she said, raising her glass, "I've brought my own. More important Alfred, you should eat something. You have to keep your strength up."

"Yes, yes, and it all looks so good."

He returned with a plate that was full, with a little bit of everything on the table. He sat in his rocker and joined the conversation.

"This has been an incredible day. I just wanted to take a last walk with Maxwell and look what happened. It turned into a Jazz Funeral with a motorcycle escort. People surrounded us, and some we didn't even know. And the music and the dancing! . . . absolutely incredible. Although I think Maxwell would have been confused by it all."

"Are you going to get another dog, Alfred?"

"I'll wait a little while before I think about that Mariposa."

The evening had come to an end. Everything was put away, and the ladies cleaned the kitchen, leaving it sparkling. Alfred took his place by the door to say good night and to thank them for their help. Taking Alfred's hand, Mariposa said good night.

"I'm right across the street should you need anything. Don't hesitate."

"Good night, Mariposa, thank you."

"I'll stop by in the morning, Alfred. Good night."

"Thanks, Ed. Good night."

"And we all take comfort in our collective grief," Roy said, following Mrs. Levi to the door.

"That's how we handle the pain and make it bearable." Mrs. Levi said, taking Alfred's hand,

"Gute Nacht Liebe."

"Good night, Mrs. Levi, thank you. . . . Thanks for everything, Roy."

"Sempre Fi buddy," he said giving him a handshake with a hug.

The house fell silent. No sound. No movement. Nothing to do. Alfred made a cup of tea and sat in his rocking chair. Staring out of the window at the twilight, Alfred dipped his tea bag, asking himself,

"Now what?"

THE OBSERVER OBSERVED

My turn.

I've had so much to say about other people, it's only right I include myself in the cast of characters. When I said everyone in Seaside was weird, I was including myself, just by the fact that I was there, although in my case it was out of necessity. After driving down from the Catskill Mts., I needed a place to stay to set myself up in Fla. I had two weeks to do that. The year before, the wife and I bought a double-wide manufactured home in Hobe Sound. A nice little bit of old Florida with an eclectic population. We wanted to be close to my soon-to-be ex-wife's parents, who were aging. Wanting to help make their lives more comfortable, as we told ourselves, we wintered in Florida to help them set up their lives so things ran smoothly.

Actually, the winters in the Catskills were becoming more difficult each year. The landscape around our Alpine Chalet on the sloping hillside, charming as it was, was difficult to navigate, with ice treacherously hiding beneath the frequent falling snow. And it was work to keep the place livable. We burned five cords of wood, plus electric base board heating to the tune of six-hundred bucks a month just to heat the place. The day began with turning on the coffee pot and feeding the remaining embers in the woodstove. If there were none, I had to start from scratch, which always seemed to take a long time when the temps were below zero. Feeding the woodstove was an all-day job. I often thought I wouldn't want to be the person in former times whose job it was to keep the fires going. There must have been hell to pay for letting the fire go out in the middle of January. Woe-be-it, not me.

And it was a full-time job. As demanding as a tyrannical mistress. Were I not to fulfill her voracious needs, she would freeze me out—casting me into the merciless cold. It was romantic at first, feeding the floor-to-ceiling fireplace and watching the snow fall beyond the windows of the chalet. Using CAD software, I designed the house, placing every light fixture, every outlet, stairway, and window to fit our lifestyle and sense of aesthetics. In the loft above, which covered half the house, was the master bedroom with a full Jacuzzi bathroom. From the balcony railing, you could view the mountain in the distance and the brook below through the trapezoid windows at the apex. Medicinal herbs grew on the north-facing hillsides. Ginseng and goldenseal, under a foot of snow, radiated their powerful presence, following the pathway to hedged herb gardens and meditation alcoves along the brook. Busts of Cicero, Herodotus, Plato, and Pythagoras sitting on top of white columns were scattered throughout the gardens. It was really grand.

But the winters were harsh and seemed to last longer each year. To compound that, my wife of twenty-five years became aware of what she was going to inherit from her parents and became completely impossible to live with. A mean, nasty, wanna-be tyrant. I was willing to tolerate all the annoyances and outbursts that come with the familiarity, but I would not live out Stephen King's *Misery*. Even when I won our petty little arguments, I was miserable. She even began to look like Cathy Bates. Yes, I understood menopausal women are difficult to deal with and are volatile, but I felt like I was swimming out to save a drowning person and was being dragged down under with them. I wanted nothing to do with it. When the snow-blower got a flat and was stuck in the snow, that was it. I immediately went to the house to start my plans. Exit, stage left.

Fortunately, I have an Angel. Angel puts thoughts in my brain and whispers advice about life in my ear. I've learned to tilt my head and listen to what Angel was telling me, and to good results. He helped me create the place we called Nimeroc, and now he was telling me to get the hell out of there. Go figure.

I packed my guns and tapestries, books, musical instruments, and my half of our pot stash. I was a little nervous about the driving, though. My proprioception[3] over the years had been changing, and my *driver's sense* sometimes became confused. I could touch my nose and all and was dexterous as hell, having studied music for years, but not so good on the highways with all the semi-trucks and crazy people scurrying about. But here I am. I made it and I think my *weird pedigree* is as good as anyone's in the Shire. So to continue……..

---

[3] Proprioception: knowing the bodies position in time and space.

PASSERSBY 2

"They say he's like the guy on that TV show, where all you see is the guy's eyes over the fence."

"That's *Tool Time*." answered someone with a woman's voice. "Margret says he talks like him, too. Says he uses the top of his jeep as a desk and works from there."

"I've heard he's a writer of some kind, he. has books in the clubhouse library."

"I heard that too. . . . Looks like they're having trouble selling that house across the street."

"Yep, it's been on the market for quite a while now."

ERIK'S FIRST GUITAR

Riding through the Shire one morning, I ran into Erik. He's a tall, thin fellow with a salt and pepper crewcut, a weathered face, and eyes that fix on you while he talks. Erik has a trunk full of stories he loves to tell, rambling and embellishing his world with incredible characters in off-beat situations. He's a comic and laughs at his own jokes. He has a Golden Retriever he calls Artemis. Most folks in the shire have GMO dogs, little dogs, some only ankle high, nervous, and hyper. You worry about stepping on them as they wrap their leash around your legs. Not Artemis. On or off the leash, she is well-behaved.

Barreling down the road on my mountain bike, I saw Artemis in the distance. She picked up a newspaper in the driveway and sat at the road's edge to wait for her owner to cross over with her. She delivered the newspaper to her neighbor's doorstep, tail wagging happily, and accepted the praise and rubs from the man as they waited by the road for me to pass.

"Now that's a dog!" I said, and we made an immediate connection. The three of us.

Artemis was a dog you felt could understand what you were saying to her, answering with her body, laughing with her tail.

"That your bike over there?" I asked, pointing to a highly polished motorcycle in the driveway across the street.

"Yup. . . . That's my baby. That's my number three."

"Number three?"

"Yup. . . . My wife, my dog, my Harley, and my guitars — in that order. That's what's important to me." A late model SUV pulls up, and a woman in her late fifties gets out.

"That's my number one. Artemis here is number two, and my guitars are number four."

"You play guitar?"

"Since I've been 'bout fourteen. Still got my first guitar. But I mostly play my Fender Strat now. Had that since 1970."

"Really! . . . Not many like that around. You've got some six-string treasures there."

"You get the drift," he said, laughing and putting out his hand. "The name is Erik. Glad to meet yah."

"Walter . . . I live in #923, over on Sandpiper. I've seen you around. Riding your Harley."

"Yah, sure. Frosty Daniels lives up the street from you. We're ridding buddies."

"So what's the make of that first guitar you were talking about?"

"That's a story in itself."

Erik's wife called out, reminding him they had an appointment at ten o'clock and they didn't want to be late.

"Okay, Betty, I'll be right along. Walt, why don't yah drop by this evening, and we'll have a beer and shoot the breeze. I'll tell yah the story 'bout my first guitar."

"Sounds good, I'll drop by around seven." Patting Artemis on the head, I was off to finish my morning ride.

My daily bike routine was to circle the park, ride over to the mailboxes to pick up the mail, and then it's back to the house to start the day's business. Takes about an hour. A routine that helps me clear the head and provides the only exercise I get during the day. After a bike ride and a shower, I'm ready for anything.

****

Erik and Betty's house is on the lake. Pastel blue, with white trim, the house is covered with bougainvillea growing on lattice, profusely flowered in purple and red. I rode over on my bike and found Erik straightening up the carport. We walked around back to a large deck that almost reached the water. They had a panoramic view of the lake. Ringed by colorful cottages with sleeping kayaks on the shore, all the activity of the lake lay before them.

"Beer-wine-Dr. Pepper, what's your pleasure?"

"I'll have a beer, thanks."

The Ibis gathered around the deck. Fishing poles stood at the ready, fastened to the corner posts. The ducks swam into the wind, creating a steady stream of ripples behind them. My host returned with the drinks.

"Plenty of birds on this side of the lake, Erik. Looks like they're all here."

"Lots of food and good hunting on this end. I get to watch the Osprey and the Eagle do their thing as well."

We sat talking, watching the day slip away. I told him how I moved from NY and had reinvented myself as a writer. "I hit the jackpot when I found Vero Beach."

"I'll drink to that!" laughed Erik, raising his glass.

"So, what's the story with the guitar?"

"Oh, yah . . . that's a good one. If you're a writer, you should write this one down."

He went on to say he grew up in an Irish neighborhood in St. Louis, Missouri. His dad had passed away a couple of years earlier, and his mom was still trying to get her bearings now that she had to take care of everything by herself. He tells his story, staring out over the lake as though he were watching pictures drift by. "She managed. Sometimes happily, sometimes chaotically. But she always did her best. Times were rough back then, and it was hard for her to relax. On the horizon, there was always an uncertain future awaiting us."

Betty brought a tray of munchies and joined us on the deck.

"Mom was pretty straightforward when she had something to say and came right to the point. This particular time, I could see she was clearly upset and aggravated."

'Erik, I got another letter from your school. This time, they want me to go down to the school for a meeting with the principal. Erik, what did you do?'

'I didn't do nothing'!'

"There's gotta' be a reason for the principle to want to speak with me. Did you get in a fight or something?"

"I ain't never been in a fight . . . at school, that is. I passed all my tests and stayed out of trouble. I even took part in class discussions. There's only a couple of days left. I don't know what this is about."

"Maybe they're going to' give you a scholarship!"

"I doubt it, Ma . . . I said I passed the tests . . . the scores weren't all that high . . . but high enough!"

"Maybe there's an award for that."

****

Next morning, Mom and I went about our usual routine silently. Neither of us were morning people and really didn't come to life until after the second cup of coffee. Our appointment was at ten o'clock, so there was no need to hurry. Not to be too early, we waited as long as we could before leaving.

'Guess I won't be needing my book bag.'

'Probably not.'

We walked to the corner to catch the local #101 bus to the school. The June sun was already warming the air, and the trees were rushing to flower. The bus came, and we got on. I sat by the window while Mom filled the coin box. The streets were a lot busier than my usual trek earlier in the morning. Shopkeepers were opening their stores and sweeping the sidewalks. People hustled along the streets with a sense of urgency. We approached a row of stores I paid special attention to every day.

'Mom... remember you said at the beginning of September that if I got through the school year, you'd get me something special for a job well done?'

'I sure do, and I meant it.'

'Well, I know what I want . . . See that pawn shop up ahead? . . . Check out the window when we pass. There! There, that guitar . . . that's what I want! I've passed by it every day since school began, watching and hoping nobody would buy it.'

'It is a pretty one . . . not like the ones the rock and rollers play.'

'I looked it up at the library. It's for playing folk music and classical stuff.'

'Do you know how much it cost?'

'No.'

'Okay, we'll talk about it again after we take care of this business.'

The rest of the way to school, I imagined myself playing my new guitar to great accolades and thunderous applause. I was eager to get started.

Everyone was in class, so the hallways were empty. I was glad because I didn't want to have to explain why my mom was at school with me. I doubled my pace and headed straight for the principal's office, mom trying her best to keep up with me. When I reached the principles door, I waited so we could go in together. She was a little winded when she introduced herself to the secretary.

'Hello, I'm Emma Czerny, and this is my son Erik. We have an appointment to see the principal.'

'Of course, Mrs. Czerny. Please, have a seat. Hello Erik. . . . I'll let monsignor Kelly know you're here, mam.'

"Oh, I forgot to mention Walt. It was a Catholic school I went to. It was believed at the time that the Catholic schools offered a better education, and though expensive, Mom wanted me to have a good start in life. We had just sat down when the Monsignor came out to greet us.

'Mrs. Czerny, so glad to meet you. Please, come into my office where we can talk.'

Monsignor Kelly had a big office with an enormous desk. Large leaded windows on one side of the room, bookshelves on the other. Behind his chair was a painting of Jesus suffering on the cross.

We all sat, and the Monsignor began.

'Mrs. Czerny, I am sorry to have to inform you we won't be accepting Erik back to Bishop Dubois H.S. next year. Issues have arisen over the past year concerning Erik's beliefs, especially in the area of religion. We feel it is causing a distraction to the rest of our students who are working hard, trying to learn the cannon of the church.'

'I don't know what you're talking about, Monsignor.'

'Erik seems to be quite taken with the religious groups in the time of Jesus. Especially the Essene sect at Qumran, where the Dead Sea Scrolls were found.'

'What scrolls? Erik, you never mentioned anything about scrolls to me.'

'I didn't think you'd be interested.'

'I'm glad he didn't learn this at home,' the monsignor said pompously. 'I am going to recommend family counseling.'

'I don't understand! . . . there's nothing' to get frightened about. They're mostly the same books that are in the bible.' I said, perhaps a little too loudly.

'Not all of them . . . some have not been sanctioned by the church.' The monsignor said, raising his voice above mine.

'So now you can include them. Maybe it was a mistake leaving them out!'

'It is not your place to determine church cannon, young man. Enough! . . . and Mrs. Czerny, then there's the matter of tuition. You are behind six months.'

'I will have that cleared up very soon, Monsignor. Certainly, before school starts in the fall. Right now, I'm borrowing from Peter to pay Paul.'

'Yes, I know your story, and you are a courageous woman for all you do. But we at Bishop Dubois have bills and responsibilities just as you do, and tuition pays the bills. Surely you understand Mrs. Czerny? You expect payment for your work, and so do we. I'm sorry, but we have already given Erik's place to a new applicant.'

'Okay . . . that ends that,' Mom said, standing. 'Please send Erik's report card to the house, and we thank you for your time, Monsignor. Erik, time to go!'

She was out the door and flew through the reception room before another word could be said. I had to hustle to keep up with her as she barreled down the hallway. By the time we reached the exit, the classroom doors opened, and the kids flooded the corridors on the way to their next class. We made it outside without being seen. I was glad, even though I was being kicked out of school, and it didn't matter. We sat at the bus stop kiosk to wait for the next bus.

'You did nothing wrong, Erik, it's their problem, not yours. I'm proud of you for studying something on your own and giving them a run for their money. What's in these scrolls that gets them so upset?'

'They just started translating them, but it looks like they are really old versions of the books that are in the bible, . . . and a couple of new ones they didn't know existed. I read about them in the archaeology magazines at the library. The Catholic scholars are afraid it will contradict church canon and want to control the translations and its release. The Jewish scholars pitch a fit and get involved, claiming the scrolls as their own. A big fight is going on.'

'You're right, I'm not interested.'

We got on the bus and sat solemnly, waiting to leave. I sat on the side where the pawnshop would be, as I did every day. There was no air-conditioning in the buses in those days, so all the windows were open. The noise from the street and the bus engine created a din that you had to talk over. Mom took my hand and smiled to console me.

'Mom, honest, it's no big deal. I really don't care. I'm glad I don't have to go back to that school. They're a bunch of dummkopfs . . . Who needs them?'

'Where do you learn this stuff?'

"The library."

The pawn shop was coming up, so I turned my attention back to the window. The guitar was still there, and I wondered if I would ever see it again, seeing as I would not be attending Bishop Dubois H.S. anymore. Mom jumped up out of her seat.

'Erik, pull the stop cord. We're getting off,' and she walked to the rear door.

'We're going to make some lemonade!'

The doors of the bus opened to the entrance of the pawnshop. We strolled in, not changing a step. The shop was empty. No one was behind the counter, and there were no sales personnel to be seen. The antiques throughout the store seemed to beckon us, all wanting to speak at the same time. Everything you could imagine was there, and some things you may have never dreamed of as well. The guitar in the window set off an amber glow. A stout, bearded man opened a curtain and greeted us.

'Good morning, how can we help you today?'

'We're interested in that guitar in the window,' Mom said, trying to sound businesslike. 'What are you asking for it?'

'We've had that guitar for quite a while . . . So long, it's become part of the decor. I can give it to you for . . . twenty-eight dollars,' he said, walking over to fetch the guitar. On the way back to the counter, he stared me in the eye and said that he knew I would make a suitable home for the *redhead*. Turning to my mom, he told her, 'Mrs. Czerny, since I don't have the documentation and there are no labels on the guitar, I can let you have it for twenty-two fifty. There are no labels or paperwork, but! . . . Son, come over here, take a look'.

Looking inside, I could see the initials J.H.T. carved into the body of the guitar.

'It could come in handy someday.' He said.

He was right. Years later, I found out that the guitar was made by a master luthier in Seville, Spain. It was his personal guitar.

We left and waited at the bus stop. I felt very proud carrying my guitar case and Mom looked proud, too. Taking our seats, I looked out of the open window to see the pawnbroker standing in his doorway.

'Mom, how did he know your name was Mrs. Czerny?

'I don't know. I didn't tell him, . . . and I paid cash money too. That guy was kind of weird, so it's best not to know what he's about.'

When we got home, I spent the rest of the day polishing and familiarizing myself with my new guitar. There was a new set of strings in the guitar case. Nylon with gold-wired bass strings, and when strung, the guitar sounded deep and mellow, with bright, rich tones. I got up early in the morning and went to the library as soon as it opened. I found a book on how to Teach Yourself to Play the Guitar in Ten Easy Lessons. Another one on how to read music, and an old battered one on music theory. I've been studying ever since."

"So, you taught yourself how to play?"

"I teach myself everything. Always have."

"That is a good story, Erik."

"I've got a million of them!"

"Well, I should head out . . . my cat is a demanding mistress and pouts when she's not fed on time."

"I know the feeling. Drop by again sometime, and I'll tell ya the story about how I got the Fender. I won it in a card game. Won it, lost it, and won it back again. It was a wild night."

"Will do. Thank you both for everything."

They wished me good night and walked me to the front of the house. I jumped on my mountain bike and headed home. The Shire looked like the set of a Disney movie. The cottages were lit up with the colored glow of the televisions, flashing like strobe lights. The moon was rising and looked heavy as the clouds drifted by. When I opened the door, the cat gave me a growl, sat in front of her bowl, and waited to be fed. I opened a can of Friskies, got myself a beer, and sat down at the computer to make notes on the newest addition to the cast of characters that peopled the Shire.

AN ANTHROPOMORPHIC OBSERVATION

There is a pair of Osprey working the lake this evening. They seem to enjoy themselves as they ride the amber solar winds. Hovering over the lake, they dive and skim the water like a stone gliding across a mirror. They look past their own reflection into the mysterious waters, searching for a glimmer of silver. The fish come to the surface looking for their own tasty morsel. The long-legged spiders walk upon the water, munching on dinner as they travel. The spider runs away, the fish returns to the abyss, and the Ospreys revisit their perch to wait for another opportunity. One of them drops down and circles the lake at a high speed, stirring the pot, so to speak. Sometimes flapping, sometimes gliding, scanning the water's surface for something shiny that can be taken home. I can see his excitement. This is what he is made for. Perfectly designed to see at great heights, he can calculate the distance and speed of his prey. He can coordinate his own movements to achieve his goal; to pluck from the grid we call space his precious sustenance. This is his tai chi, and he is firing on all eight.

"You'll not get away this time, silver food."

A bass has come close to the surface. He doesn't see any shadows on the glass ceiling, so he swims along happily, feasting on a cornucopia of tasty insects. There is no wind today. The water is calm, not a ripple, except for the bugs on the surface. Perfect!

The osprey whistles then dives feet first towards the earth. Thirty... thirty-five... forty... forty-five miles an hour, he plunges fearlessly. The bass sees his shadow, but it is too late. Wide-eyed and helpless, he is yanked from the water.

"I can't breathe … there is nothing here to breathe." He silently screams, squirming, losing consciousness with each moment. Suddenly, he is falling. An eagle has tried to steal the osprey's prey. Feet first, back against the wind, almost upside-down, the eagle stretches out his long talons to reach the bass but fails to catch him. The bass slaps the water with a belly-flop, shocking him once again, but the water filling his gills brings life.

"I can breathe, I can breathe!" slowly coming back, gaining momentum, mustering the strength to dive deep below the surface where he will be safe. Then, a pair of talons snatches him from the water.

"No!... not again! I can't breathe. Where are you taking me? It's cold here. Oh shit! There are more of them. Don't put me in there. Stop... there eating me. You're not supposed to eat me. Where are the big ones? At least they don't eat meeeeee......"

The fledgling osprey chirp wildly in the nest as they feast upon their silver treat. Mom and Dad fly off into the orange glow. Returning to work one more time before nightfall.

RAYMOND'S BATH-HOUSE

Raymond lived next door, on the east side of my house. A gregarious fellow, seemingly ingenuous with a friendly deportment. He moved to Florida from Connecticut to help his elderly parents, who lived closer to the ocean on Orchard Island. He was very proud of the purchase of his house. Like mine, it was built in the seventies, so he probably paid around twenty thousand dollars for it. Newer models here at Seaside start at $120,000, moving higher along the lake.

"My parents can't believe how little I paid for it," he told me when we first met. "My father wants to buy several houses to use as rental properties."

Raymond was tall, mid-fifties, with a shadow beard and a bald head. He was very upbeat and confident in his prospects. He raved about Vero Beach and Seaside Park, reciting a litany of their amenities.

"There's the ocean and the opera — Art museums and galleries — all kinds of music, including a symphony. And it's so safe, too!" Evidently, crime in Connecticut was beginning to percolate and there was little there to hold him.

Raymond went to work making the new place his own. He strung patio lights along the eaves, filled the planter boxes with colorful shrubs, hung baskets of flowers, and placed rainbow welcome mats in front of the doors. He screened in a portion of the carport, lining the walls with bamboo curtains and Tiffany lamps. The new eight-cylinder black pickup truck he swapped for his Subaru, barely fit in the driveway.

Raymond had two small black dogs he walked several times a day. They were nasty little dogs, mean and pugnacious. Standing at his feet, bearing their fangs, they exuded a violent contempt for anyone trying to enter their world. It was that way wherever they went. He constantly corrected them. Totally the opposite of Raymond himself. He was the perennial nice guy. Always willing to help. One time, he brought me chicken soup when he heard I was under the weather. I wasn't, but the soup was really good. He'd watch people's homes when they were out of town, feeding the fish or watering the plants. During the covid scare, he shopped and ran errands for his parents and sometimes their friends. Mostly, everybody loved Raymond. Mostly, except for the time he overheard some nasty comments about the Biden signs on his front lawn. He put them away, not wanting any kind of confrontation. Another time, someone reported him to the office for parking in his dead neighbor's driveway.

" I told her, . . . 'Phyllis, and why do you care about who parks where?'"

Raymond had acquired a southern, almost theatrical accent. Holding his leashed dogs as though they were a team of horses, he would gesture with his free hand like a Roman orator, stating his position with flamboyant language. A friend was staying with him (a person who never came out of the house and was a bit of a mystery, according to Alabama) and he needed the parking space for his guest. He made his case to everybody along the way while on his walks. The dogs were mean, but everyone enjoyed talking with Raymond. The troglodyte finally surfaced to scrub the oil stains left in the driveway by his battered Mercedes Sedan. His name was Jerry. Alabama befriended him and he was deemed okay, taking a place himself in the cast of characters that populated Seaside.

Raymond landed a job as a dispatcher for an Air conditioning company, which he was very happy with. He liked the 401k, the benefits, and the credit union, which he promptly used to buy a new A.C. system.

"Things have really fallen into place for you, man," I said, congratulating his good fortune.

"Moving to Florida was the best thing I've ever done," he shouted, moving down the street. Beyond all the theatrics and drama, Raymond was a happy man.

Once he started a work routine, he didn't stop by the truck to talk as often. I'd catch him in the evenings occasionally, walking the demons that barked and snarled at his feet. He'd fill me in with the latest news and then move on down to the dog park.

He liked to entertain. I'd come home at night, and the street would be lined with cars. I could hear folks drinking and laughing and enjoying themselves while I ate my dinner. He didn't have his parties too often, so it never became an annoyance and brought a little life to an otherwise sleepy street. He bought himself a golf cart that he would zip about the community, visiting friends, the clubhouse, the pool, and the dog park. A lot of socializing was done at the dog park. Anything you wanted to know about the community could be found there; and some things that were not posted on the bulletin board at the clubhouse.

Raymond befriended a guy who lived on the other side of the park. He sported a Fu Manchu mustache and helped with the renovation of his house. I had seen the Fu Manchu guy in the park, riding in his golf cart with a red kayak and fishing pole on the roof, ready to go at a moment's notice. We went to the same barbershop, and I'd overhear him boasting about being able to out-kayak his grandkids. Sounded like a big outdoorsman. He'd lived at Seaside for several years, taking care of his mother and enjoying his retirement. The scuttle-butt was that back after the 2017 Category five hurricane, he was busted for growing Cannabis in his shed. The police found his grow while making their wellness checks after the storm. He told the judge the marijuana was to soothe his mother's arthritic pain and not for any nefarious purpose. Not being a threat to the community, he was placed on probation and had to perform 250 hours of community service.

Raymond bought a Jacuzzi and placed it in the screened portion of his carport. He'd have friends over on Sundays for barbeque and a soak. They'd whoop it up, laughing and splashing, eating and telling jokes. There was always a lot of traffic on South Sandpiper on those days, with people walking and driving by the party house to catch a glimpse of what was going on. He had a diverse group of friends; White-Black-Hispanic-Asian. Tall, short, round and bald, a good time was had by all. After their soak, they'd grab their beach hats and towels and head for the pool. Walking single file like ducks in a row, they'd wave and say hello to everyone along the way. It was quite a show, like something from "La Cage Aux Folles."

I had not talked to Raymond for a while. I'd see his truck in the driveway occasionally, but we never spoke. Evidently, he met someone, and they were going to move in together. Alabama had stopped by the truck and filled me in.

"You should have seen him riding in the golf cart with his boyfriend. He looked like a blushing bride in a horse-drawn buggy, riding through town so everybody could see em'." Alabama was genuinely happy for Raymond, almost proud. A couple of days later, the *For Sale* signs were put up. It took a while, but the place was sold, and Phil D. Pipe and his wife Sassy, moved in. But that's another story.

ESTER VAN HOVEN

Walking down the center of the road, an old lady with a cane calculated her steps. Determined, rising up and down, she made her way along the road. She wore a tweed jacket and pants and sported a wide-brimmed canvass hat that looked warm but more suited to a New York winter than Florida. I pulled slowly alongside her and asked if she needed help.

"I'm going to the office to pay my rent."

"Can I give you a ride?"

"Thank you. God bless you.

I got out and helped her into the Jeep. "Jesus sent you to me," she said as she made her best effort. It was difficult for her, and it took a while, so traffic backed up behind us and people were getting annoyed. When we pulled up to the office, she asked me to make out the check for her. I frowned and told her it was bad practice to allow anyone to have access to her checkbook unless she really trusted them. The name on the check was Ester Van Hoven.

"Here," I said, handing her back the checkbook, "you're the only one who should sign this." She slowly signed it and gave it back to me with a look suggesting I should deliver it.

"I'll be right back," I said realizing that it would take forever to walk her to the office and back again.

In the office, I explained to the receptionist that I was delivering Ester's check. She was a Hispanic woman, pretty, with a broad smile and an affected, obsequious demeanor. I asked her if there was anything that could be done to help the old girl out.

"Maybe you can send someone over to her house to pick up the check or something. She was gonna' walk here, all the way from South Sandpiper."

She shook her head and frowned.

"No, there's nothing we can do. Ms. Van Hoven has many needs and should have her children to help her. If we do things for her, we would have to do them for everybody. I'm sorry, there is nothing we can do."

****

"Well . . . that's done," I said, getting back into the jeep, "I'll give you a ride home."

"I have to go to the AT&T store to pay my phone bill. They say they're going to cut off my telephone. I don't understand."

"Where's the store?"

"Right down Twentieth Street."

"I think I know the one. Well then, we should get started." She nodded, and we were on our way. As we passed a church along the roadway, Ester started bouncing up and down, raising her clasped hands to the sky.

"That's my church. That's where I go to pray to Jesus."

A big church, modern in style, with an enormous parking lot I have seen full to capacity on Sunday mornings. Written on the marquee, in bold gold letters, was: COME WORSHIP WITH PASTOR BUDDY — SERVICES AT 9 AND 12.

"Do you go on Sundays?" I asked.

"Yes, and on Wednesday, too." She said, tucking her hair into her hat. "Pastor Buddy sends a van to pick us up. He knows Jesus personally."

When we arrived at the AT&T store, she gave me her bill and the checkbook which I filled out before we both went inside. The salesman recognized and greeted Ester. He brought up her account on his computer, printed out the bill, and gave it to her to examine. She checked his bill with hers, and with her nod of approval, he gave her a pen to sign the check. This was a routine they had played out before. The salesman told me that Ester showing up had become a monthly occurrence.

"She doesn't have a computer or understand how to pay on her phone, so she has to come down to the store to make her payment. The system is set up for a more tech-savvy customer, and folks without tech skills get lost in the *'nowhere.'*" The world had moved on, leaving Ester behind.

When we got back in the Jeep, Ester made yet another request.

"Can we make one more stop? I always go to Walmart for a few things before going home."

Getting a little annoyed, I snapped at her, "Okay. Sure, but I have my own errands to run, so we can't do a big shopping." I immediately felt like a heel for not wanting to help an old woman get food for the house.

She didn't need to do a big shopping; she needed a toasted pretzel with mustard. Her steps quickened as we walked through the sliding doors at Walmart, heading straight for the food court.

"I'll have two pretzels with mustard on the side, please."

I sat with her at a small bistro table as she savored the Coney Island pretzel. She asked me several times, while licking her fingers, if I wanted one, assuring me it was her treat. She ate one pretzel, then carefully wrapped the other in a napkin along with the packets of Gulden's mustard. This was Ester's ambrosia.

On the ride back home, she asked me to pray to Jesus with her, saying it was only with His help that we could get through this life and return to our maker. She clasped her hands together, closed her eyes intently, and spoke to Jesus.

"Please, Lord, help this man find his way through this turbulent world so he can return to your grace." She became excited, passing Pastor Buddy's church again, saying that God was merciful, having sent Pastor Buddy to shepherd his flock. Once again, I realized how important religion was in our world. What would people do if they didn't have their faith in God?

I asked her if she had kids or family that could help with business matters and run errands. She said she had a daughter but that her daughter was mad at her.

"I was only trying to protect her. I warned her about wicked men and what they wanted when she was small. She says I ruined her life, and now she can't have a normal relationship. I was only trying to protect her."

"Have you any other family in the area, Ester?"

"No, they're all up north. My son comes to see me sometimes, but not for a long time. That's my house, just up the road. I live at number 225."

I pulled into the carport and helped her out of the Jeep. She grasped my hand and squeezed it, saying, "Jesus loves you."

The house was kind of stark, with no signs that anyone was living there. Weeds were growing in the planter boxes, and the house needed painting. I gave her my business card and told her to call me if an emergency came up. Maybe not such a good idea, because a couple of days later I got a call. She wasn't on my contact list, so it went to voice mail.

"Hello, I know you don't know me but I'm a friend of Ester's. I'm here visiting her and have to go home, but it's raining. My dog is sick, and I've got to get to her. Can you give me a ride? Ester said you were a wonderful person and would help me." A second call came soon after.

"Hello, it's me again. I've got to get home, but it's still raining. My dog is sick, and I have to go to her." I didn't listen to the call until hours later when I would be of no help, so I let it go.

I've seen Ester around since then, getting into people's cars and going about her business. I wave, smile, and drive by, feeling guilty about avoiding her.

****

Ruby, the woman who cuts my hair, also lives in Seaside and we exchange stories whenever I'm in her chair. We live on opposite sides of the park and share the different bits of gossip we hear from our neighbors. I told her about an old lady that I had picked up walking down the center of the road. "I wound up driving her all over Vero."

She stopped cutting my hair, leaned over, stared into my eyes through the mirror, and gasped.

"I picked her up too. I brought her to Walmart to do some shopping, and she bought me a pretzel. Made me put mustard on it. Looked strange . . . but it was pretty good!"

"Same here only I didn't go for the pretzel. Her name is Ester. I haven't seen her lately, have you?"

"She's in an assisted living home. The family finally stepped in to help out. After driving her home, I helped with taking in the groceries and was horrified. The place was filthy. Mold everywhere, dishes piled up in the sink, bugs crawling on the countertops. You could hardly see out of the windows. They were so dirty. All of her belongings were in boxes scattered along the floor."

"Holy shit!" I said as she resumed cutting my hair.

"I asked her if she had family that could help her. She said they were mad at her for a long time and never call, *'that's why I have the phone. In case they call.'* There was a name and phone number on the refrigerator: Damien Van Hoven, (212) 737-0507. I copied the info into my phone and asked her if I could call him. She agreed, *'but it won't do any good.'"*

"Wow, that's sad," I said, feeling guilty again. Ester always made me feel guilty.

"Well, that's not all, there's more. I called her son, and I guess it embarrassed him because he told me the whole story. Ester filed for divorce about twenty years ago, claiming her husband had molested his daughter. It was an ugly episode that tore the family apart. The husband was cleared, and the family rallied around him, disgusted at what she had done.

'My mother has never been right.' he whined.

The divorce went through, the family disowned her, and she became homeless. He said he would receive a telephone call from time to time from the city services for the homeless, but she didn't want their help, and nothing ever came of it. She lived in the subway at the Port Authority on 42nd Street in Manhattan for years." He talked loudly and sounded very upset. *'I found her there a couple of times and tried to talk some sense into her, but it didn't do any good. She told me she couldn't leave because of the pretzels they sold at the bus station. She lived on them. She said that her grandma used to take her to Coney Island on weekends. She would buy pretzels with mustard, and they would sit together on the boardwalk and watch the waves playing with the shore. She said it was the best time of her life.'*

"Wow, this is like some Greek tragedy, Ruby." She was done cutting my hair but made a snip here and there as she continued with the story.

"The husband died and to everyone's surprise, left money in the will to take care of Ester. The son was made executor with the stipulation that she receive the help she needed. He bought a place at Seaside for her and set up a bank account with a monthly allowance.

'She has plenty of money. There's no reason she can't pay her bills. She thinks everyone is trying to cheat her 'cause she's old. I've flown down there a couple of times to check on her, but . . . but I haven't been able to get away for a while.'

"Well, the kids did step up and found her a place at an assisted living home in Sebastian. That's why you haven't seen her for a while."

"I hope they have Coney Island pretzels there."

She laughed, brushing the hair cuttings from my shoulders. "That part of the story is sweet."

"She'll find a way to get her pretzels. One thing for sure about Ester is that she uses whatever resources she has at hand to get what she wants. That business about walking down the center of the road was brilliant."

"How was she able to survive all those years being homeless?"

"I'll bet she found a niche in the bus station and set herself up nice. All she needed money for was the pretzels."

"I guess she could get that by panhandling, but the winters are so cold."

"She's a very smart lady. She survived using her wits. Ester is a genius at being homeless."

On the way to the cash register, we turned a few heads that had zeroed in on our conversation. I paid Ruby for the haircut, and we agreed to keep each other informed should anything new develop in Ester's saga. I suggested we meet up at Seaside's happy hour to raise a glass to the old girl. Ruby looked concerned.

" I hope she's alright. I think I'll check up on her and make sure she has her pretzels."

"She's brilliant." I said, "The old girl still has us all working for her." I smiled and left feeling sure of Ester's prowess.

PASSERSBY 3

Dogs cannot pass my house without leaving their marker on my front lawn. It's as though it were mandatory. A bearded burley fellow walks by with his Dachshund. His companion, a tall, thin guy with a mustache, is wearing a Vero Beach baseball cap. He walks a Maltese so small it gets lost behind potted plants.

"She says you piss like a racehorse. Says you leave your bathroom window wide open just so she can hear ya. She thinks you're trying to seduce her," the stout fellow with the Dachshund said.

"That's crazy! You're making this up," as the Maltese dug into the lawn.

"That's what the wife tells me, and I can believe it." The Dachshund has found the Norfolk pine and waters it. "That woman ain't right in the head. I don't hardly know how Charlie can stand being married to her."

"I should talk with Charlie. Tell him it's not true!"

"He already knows that. He told me he'd pay yah just to take her off his hands. Maybe you should think about it. You've been single a couple of years now, ain't yah?"

"You're crazy!"

"She's a handful, but Charlie says she's as feisty as a filly let loose for the first time come spring. Said she gave a good blow job too . . . Something to consider?"

"You're as crazy as she is. . . . What a picture that makes. The woman's arms are as big as my thigh. And it's all muscle. . . . I have to go," he said, pulling his reluctant beast after him.

"Aw, come on, Smedley. . . . I'm just having fun with it. You're the only one I know who can seduce women just by draining the hog.

THE MUSCA

Riding my bike on a clear December morning, I stopped to talk with some neighbors who were taking their power walks. They told me Abraham Levinson had passed away. He was seventy-eight years old and died with a fly swatter in his hand, spread-eagle on the kitchen floor. He lay dead for several days, and maggots spewed from every orifice. There would be a pot-luck memorial to pay homage to the old boy at the clubhouse on Saturday. All were invited to attend. Abe was ornery, but he was a good guy and was well-liked.

Continuing my ride, I imagined his last day on earth. It played out in my mind like a movie; I almost hit a parked car. I knew Abe pretty well, so it was easy to fill in the frames.

"You son of a bitch, I'm gonna get ya (wapp) . . . stand still!. . . (wapp) The only way you're getting out of here alive is if you leave the way you came. (wip-wip) That's right, head for the door. No! Not the sink, the door (wapp). Fucking flies, you come inside and never leave."

Abe does his best to follow the fly as it darts from the sink to the table to the garbage can.

"You're quite the trapeze artist, hey, (wip-wip) a regular Burt Lancaster.

(wapp) . . . Stand still, damn it!"

He loses sight of the fly. Searching every corner of the kitchen, he cannot find his elusive prey and goes to his computer to look up this adept, acrobatic enemy. Armed with new knowledge, he resumes his search, finding the Musca in the living room.

"There you are, you little bastard. Standstill (wip-wip). Quite a pedigree you have, my little friend. Sixty-six million years' worth. (wapp) But don't let it go to your head. The best you can do is live for a month. I don't know how old you are, (wapp) but you're not going to reach my age."

The fly leads him around the room. From the chair to a painting, the window to the refrigerator, he jumps from one location to another effortlessly. The Musca's red eyes and black body stand out on the white wall, shaking his wings as though laughing.

"You're taunting me, aren't you? You shit-eating low life. I'm gonna spread your guts all over this wall. (zap) You've got all those millions of years, my friend, but I've got Wikipedia! You're doomed!" (wapp)

Evading the swats of his determined stalker, the fly passes through the kitchen door, with Abe following him.

"So, this is your preferred battleground, hey. I agree. This is our O.K. Corral. It is here the victor will be revealed. Monsieur Musca domestica, 'Prends garde a toi'! (wapp)

Frustrated, he chases the fly about the kitchen. Like a kid in a playground playing tag, the fly appears to be enjoying himself with complete abandon.

"I've only got two legs, and stiff as they may be, you're no match for me! (snip-snip). My cousin Isaac is an exterminator, you know. Bugs die wherever he goes. Like the Visigoths, nothing is left in his wake (wapp). Sons of bitches, (snip) daughters of father rapers, (snip) you're all garbage (wapp). . .

I don't think I'll be needing him for just you though. Besides, he charges too much. You think he would have a discount for family, but no, not Isaac!" (wapp)

The Musca continues to elude Abe, pulling him from one end of the room to the other, finally landing on the screen door.

"That's the idea. Here, I'll even open it for you."

The fly hoovers about the door. Up-down, left-right.

"Make up your mind! In or out. Let's get crackin'. I haven't got all day to play these games with you.".

The Musca flies out only to return a moment later with another fly.

"You son of a bitch! You're playing me. Who's that? Reinforcements? Must be a girlfriend. She's a lot bigger than you. (swat) That's not gonna help."

Abe swats at them as they dart from one side of the room to the other. They maneuver like navy test pilots, banking sharp turns, rising to the ceiling only to come to rest on the floor.

"Ah! the girlfriend has found the cat bowl!" (wapp)

With a rush of adrenaline, he swats at the fly and the cat food scatters across the floor. Chasing the girlfriend, Abe slips on the kibble and winds up on his ass. Humbled, he gets up slowly.

"Round one . . . Ouch, you work well together. Ugg, did ya learn that in flight school?

Standing straight, he arranges his clothes and resumes his pursuit.

"There you are. (swat) Yeah, I know it's you. You've got them beady little eyes. Stand still, you cross-eyed little bastard. (wip) Wikipedia says you see in slow motion. What kind of way is that to live? (swat) So you think your proprioception is better than mine, aye. We'll see about that. I'm just getting started. (wapp)

Abe is relentless, chasing one fly, then the other. He swats frantically all about the room, crushing the kibble under his feet along the way. Tiring, he takes a seat at the table and surveys the mess in the kitchen. Salt, pepper, and other condiments are scattered along the countertop. The cat's bowl lies on the other side of the room, with the kibble strewn across the floor. The tablecloth is half off the table, and his coffee mug sits precariously on its edge. It was, in fact, a war zone. The Musca sits on the edge of the coffee cup, rubbing his feet together. Abe laughs, slapping his leg. "

"You're a cheeky bastard, I'll say that." For a few moments Abe enjoys the fly's company.

"You cleaning your feet expecting to help yourself to some more of my food? Do you think you've won or something? I don't think so, my friend. Yeah, I know it's you. I can tell by your size and them long legs. You tired, too? You ain't moving. Taking a little rest, are ya? The internet says you've been following my people around since the beginning. We took you across the world with us. I think you might show a little appreciation and mosey on outside. Take that girlfriend with you. I don't want her laying any eggs around here. Go on. The door is still open. There ain't no shit or carrion or rotten food lying around here. There's a great, big beautiful world outside just waiting for you. So, what's it going to be?" The fly continues to groom his feet. "I thought so!" (wapp)"

Abe gets up from his chair, closes the door, and returns to the table with the swatter raised high. He swings wildly, knocking the coffee cup to the floor. The female Musca lands on the shattered cup and soaks up the residue left in it with her proboscis.

(wapp) "On your way, little lady, I'll deal with you later."

The old man searches for his prey throughout the kitchen. Not finding him, he checks the living room, but still no sign of him.

"Oh Beelzebub, . . . where are you? Or should I call you Beelze-bug? Show yourself. We have business to finish. You can't hide forever. (swat) It's time to meet your maker." Returning to the kitchen, he takes a swipe at the female with no expectations of hitting her. "Where is the 'Lord of the Flies'? Tell your consort to show himself! His moment of reckoning has come. We will put an end to this once and for all. Then I'll come back for you."

Abe finds his nemesis scavenging on the stovetop.

"There you are, you little bastard." He rushes to the stove, flyswatter raised to deliver its death blow. His heart is racing. Abe slips on the kibble again, this time hitting his head on the edge of the table. He falls face down onto the floor, swatter in hand and loses consciousness. He lies motionless, bleeding from a head wound. The room is still, almost silent. Only the sound of the buzzing wings of the Musca penetrates the void.

Mrs. Anderson had not seen her neighbor for several days. Abe usually busied himself working about the house, and she was concerned. After ringing the bell and not receiving an answer, she called EMS for a wellness check-up. She was with them when they entered, finding Abe on the floor in a pool of blood, gripping the fly swatter. Flies hovered about the body. Poor Mrs. Anderson. They were friends and neighbors, and now she would have to live the rest of her days remembering the last time she saw Abe.

I brought ribs and baked beans to the memorial. They were Abe's favorites.

IAN MCDERMOTT

I play pool with Ian on Tuesday afternoons. We'll have lunch at the clubhouse, then spend the rest of the afternoon struggling to make the billiard balls behave. Neither of us is a very skillful player, but we manage to sink a few, sometimes making rather surprising shots. Ian is a jovial fellow, in good shape, and looks young for his age. He has lived in the Shire for over a decade and is the go-to historian for all the newbies to Seaside. He eats well, works out in the gym, and is on every committee in the park. With a full head of hair, some of it the original red, he stands sure of himself, straight as an arrow. But something impish in his manner betrays the fact that behind those green eyes lives a leprechaun. Half the time, you didn't know whether or not he was being serious.

We met up on a gloomy, chilly day in late October. It was overcast and windy, reminding us that winter does exist in Florida. Ian was as somber as the day outside the window. His voice had dropped, and his manner was completely serious. The television was on, tuned to MSNBC.

"I don't understand what the hell they're saying when they start talking about

'Privilege'. It's like some three-card Monte scam on a street corner. The only privilege I had was I could stay out of jail if I wanted."

Racking up the balls and pointing to the TV, he looked disgusted. "They talk as though everyone but them had a charmed life. No one I knew growing up had it easy. We all struggled. It was always one thing or another. I personally have had PTSD since I've been six years old." Chalking his cue stick, he stood at the window, staring into the fog churning on the lake. "Those of my friends who survived the neighborhood had to carve out a life for themselves, with very few options to choose from. You did good if you worked for the city and became a fireman or sanitation worker with a steady job and a pension. People still talked about the depression and the war as though it were recent history." Pointing his cue stick at the TV screen, "Turn that thing off, will ya, Walt? Hard to concentrate with all that babbling going on . . . I'll break first." He bent over the table, strategically placed his hands, and sent the balls spiraling into chaos. "Just like them, pool balls. Once everything is set in motion, you have to make something from what you've got. Five-ball, right side pocket." The five-ball banked off two corners, just missing the called pocket. "Sometimes you don't make it, but you keep trying."

"Jim Crow was ugly, Ian; I've seen it myself," I said, studying the table. "Nine-ball, right corner."

"Ugly as sin! I'm right there with you," he shouted just as I was taking my shot. "Back in the day, I was at all the rallies to put an end to that shit. Doesn't mean everybody's life was a cake-walk. That's stupid."

"And the nine-ball did not find the corner! . . . What did you mean when you said you've had PTSD since you were six?"

"I recognized it in one of my earliest memories. One night, my old man was drunk and fighting with my mother and older brothers about which television show they would watch. He wanted to watch William F. Buckley, and they wanted to watch Red Skelton. He was waving his arms, yelling that he paid for everything and he was the boss. The old man threatened to throw the TV out of the window, and I was terrified it would hit someone on the street below. I cried into my pillow that night, not to be heard. Eleven-ball, left side pocket. Next day, my younger brother and I were playing with a large box on the sidewalk. We pretended it was our castle, and inside, we were safe from the world. A young couple passed by and stopped to talk with us.

'Look at how cute they are,' she said with a big smile. I think she was in a maternal way. Then she lost her smile. Her face slowly changed, and I could see all the pain I didn't know I had. She saw two little boys frozen, traumatized by life, in shock. She said she wanted to hug us but kept her distance. As they walked away, she turned and looked back. She was dazzling, like a princess in a Disney movie. My brother and I called her 'Lovely Lady' and talked about her often, wondering if she would stop by again. I didn't know it was called PTSD, but I knew I had something. I saw it in her eyes."

Ian was slipping in and out of his New York dialect, engrossed in a story he needed to tell.

"Back then, there was always something that turned the world upside-down. A few years after that, I was walking home from school with my friends, and there's the old man arguing with the superintendent of the building, and all of our furniture piled up at the curb." Ian bent over confidently to take his shot, "I'll take your nine-ball and place it in the side pocket," and in it went, along with the twelve-ball.

"You like the side pockets, I see."

"That I do. Three ball, left-hand corner." He didn't make it and retreated to the window. Making ready for my next shot, I asked him, "So what did you do? How did it end up? Ten-ball, right corner." I scratched.

"Better luck next time, Walt. . . . Well, the old man paid the rent, and we moved everything back inside. That's five floors, mind you, no elevator. Happened more than once, too. Fourteen-ball, left-hand corner. But we weren't the only ones. Other kids in the neighborhood had the same problem. One time I saw a family cooking dinner right there on the sidewalk. They slept on the couch and in the chairs for days before they got everything straightened out. We weren't the only ones by any means. Things were booming, but not everybody caught on." He chalked up and studied the table. "Five-ball banked off this side and into the opposite side pocket." He made the shot and walked around the table.

"Our lives were different back then. If a policeman caught you being rowdy, he'd reprimand you and then take you to the priest, who, after a lecture, would call your parents, where it became a surety you would get a slap on the back of the head, being an embarrassment to the family and all. Corporal punishment was common in those days. At home, in the schools, and no one even thought there was anything wrong with it. I knew that that world was not for me. Four-ball, straight ahead. After school, I worked odd jobs, carrying people's groceries home from the A&P, helping paint apartments, anything for a buck. Fifteen-ball far corner. By the time I graduated high school, I'd saved enough money to move to Florida and re-invent myself. Two ball, left-hand corner." Ian was on a roll and kept talking. "I started off selling anything I could at flea markets and County Fairs until I saved enough to open a hardware store." The balls clacked as he continued. "Met the wife, had kids and over the years built a big house and a thriving business. I don't recall anyone giving me anything. Three-ball, right where I'm standing."

"What the hell happened since the last time we played? I've never seen you run the table like this before." He ignored me and continued. "The same story for my brother, Michael. He worked for the sanitation department during the day and studied law at City College at night. Any free time he had, he was studying at the library on Forty-second Street. Six-ball, right-hand corner. It took him years to finish, but he did it. Nobody gave him nothin' but a job. And don't believe for a minute that all lawyers are rich. Just ain't so. He has a pleasant house, a pretty wife, and a practice over in Tampa. But he ain't rich. Thirteen-ball right where you're standing." He missed, and I finally got a chance to clear some of the balls left on the table. Ian stood at the window, studying the lake as he continued his story.

"Don't get me wrong, I'm not complaining. I just don't like being gaslighted, is all. They're rewriting history right before our eyes. I've had a good life, no doubt about it. We were born in a prosperous time, in a country where a person could make something of themselves. That's about as good as it gets for working people. But it doesn't mean it was easy. There were a lot of twenty-hour days and sleepless nights along the way. Oh . . . is it my turn? One ball, right-hand corner."

His spirit lifted with each successful shot. "Not complaining at all. Hell, I've been to the pyramids, danced in the Colosseum of Rome, and sang 'New York New York' in the ancient amphitheater at Ephesus. It's been a wild ride, I have to say. We've had our share of happiness and our share of tragedy. Having said that, Walt, I'll put the eight-ball in the corner pocket." And in it went. "Rack them up, lad, and get ready to lose again. . . . Looks like it's clearing up out there on the lake."

We played two more games, and he won both. Ian was full of himself and pranced around the table like a peacock. Occasionally, he spoke with a brogue, complaining about student loans, foreign policy, and free speech. His wife Stella poked her head in, asking him if he was about ready to go.

"Be right with ya luv. . . . Well, Walt, I think I'm gonna quit while I'm ahead. He took his cue stick apart and placed it in its case. "I have thoroughly enjoyed taking you to the cleaners today, and I guess you learned a lot about me." He even laughed with a brough, "And all of it is true. I'll See ya later, buddy. I'm off to eat a leg of lamb and then make love to me wife. Same time next week?"

After that game, I saw Ian in an entirely new light. We've played many times since, but he has never talked about himself or the past in such a way. He was back to his congenial old self, telling comical stories about the goings on in the Shire. Having seen much of what he talked about myself, I agreed with him. The building I grew up in could have been the set for the 'Honeymooners.' There was a kindred spirit thing going on, carried by a tacit understanding of the world. Something other folks, someone from West Virginia, might not fully understand. Their stories of walking miles to school in shoes with holes in them are gripping, but they don't have the same 'Paisan' quality of a crowded, dirty city story. I have the same kind of simpatico with Senor Sanchez. Everyone has a tale to tell in the Shire.

TRISHA

Trisha has straight purple hair sometimes. At other times, she might have beaded braids or Rasta man dreadlocks. She is a short, stout black woman, always changing the way she looks, wearing colorful clothes and fully accessorizing. She must have a dozen pairs of sneakers to match her outfits. You can see and hear her a block away. She walks her Yorkshire Terriers past the house and occasionally stops to chat about life, the weather, and the goings on in the Shire.

"Someone took a dump in the pool and left a turd floating around in it. Now, it's going to take two days to disinfect the water. They closed the dog park last month for the same reason. Someone is not picking up after their dog, and the office chained the gate to teach us a lesson. We seem to have a real waste disposal problem here at Seaside, and I intend to bring it up at the next meeting."

Trisha is a real people person. Talks to anyone who will listen. She ran for and was elected to the board of the homeowner's association but left at the year's end, frustrated was she by the tepid response to her innovative ideas about how things should be run at Seaside. She was always championing one cause or another.

"I can't stand injustice! I don't care what it is, LGBT, climate, or anything else. I'm gonna fight for what's right."

I was at a meeting where she got up and demanded that everyone should be made to follow the same rules regarding the size of dogs permitted in the park.

"There are people walking around here with large breeds of dogs, just walking along like they're doing nothing wrong, without a care in the world. Are some people at Seaside getting special treatment over others?"

The manager at the time was a retired military guy named Lincoln. This was his second career, and he saw for himself a future with the large corporation that owned so many communities in the area and nationwide, knowing they would always be in need of organized, disciplined management. In the beginning, he attempted to run a tight ship. He began by enforcing the parking rules. No parking on the grass and no overnight parking on the street, with threats of being towed at the owner's expense. He had laid down the gauntlet. Throughout the community, he posted flyers and sent emails informing the residents that four-sided inspections of the homes would now take place throughout the year. Failure to comply with the inspection as per the signed contract would lead to legal action and possible eviction. If he tells you your house needs painting, you'd better comply or else the attorneys would be contacting you. You had thirty days to complete the tasks. It was unnecessary, for the most part. People loved their Shire homes and took good care of them.

Dealing with ornery, cantankerous, retired residents was like herding cats. There was nothing in the military code of conduct he could look to for guidance, and he had to wing it. He lightened up over time and became more congenial. But he kept the place looking snappy, repairing roads and replacing street signs and lamp posts. Personally, I was glad there was some organization running things at Seaside; without it, our Shire could become a barrio in a matter of years. But I digress.

I got a kick out of watching Trisha debate Lincoln. A cameo of the firebrand and the stoic. A repeat of Fredrick Douglass and President Lincoln. He answered her calmly, explaining the rules governing the size of canine pets.

"First of all, if they are service dogs or comfort dogs," Lincoln said, "they are exempt from the size rules in our community contract. Service animals are likely to be of the larger breeds. When was the last time you saw a chihuahua working as a seeing-eye dog? Although comfort dogs can be any size, often they are of the larger breeds. So . . . the people walking their dogs have nothing to feel guilty about. They are protected by law. I hope that answers your question." Trisha sat back down and was quiet for the rest of the meeting.

Her husband was the complete opposite of Trisha. He didn't want to be bothered by anybody and barely acknowledged you when you passed him walking the dogs or at the mailbox. He carried himself with the bearings of a man who had heard and seen it all and didn't need replays. Trisha once told me they moved down from the D.C. area, and I suspect they both had healthy career pensions from the government. They retired to sunny Florida to enjoy the *salt life*. They fixed up their place (winning *the House of the Month* first year at Seaside), covering every square inch of the lot with flowers and lawn ornaments. The lot sizes at Seaside are little more than a postage stamp, and it always amazes me how many gnomes, pelicans, alligators, and flower pots people can cram onto their lots. I myself prefer the rabbits and squirrels, ducks and Ibis freely walking about.

After finishing the work on the house, there came the '*now what are we going to do?*' moments. In the first year after moving to Florida, people are up early and at the beach, sometimes to watch the sunrise. Then cycling through the community, greeting the neighbors, taking a morning swim, maybe followed by a round of golf before dinner and drinks. Absolutely brilliant! But as time rolls on, it becomes routine. Some people need more to do. Trisha's husband found a job with Treasure Coast Security and she volunteered, assisting the underserved communities in the area. He drove a company car and passed the house every morning at 7:30. She'd pass soon after in her red Honda Civic, the bumper covered with Obama stickers and the back seat full of flyers. Evidently, they hired someone in the community to walk the Yorkies.

I didn't see much of Trisha for long periods at a stretch, and when I did, she'd tell me about all the community projects she was involved in. Trisha didn't just talk about things, she did something about it. She said she and her husband were talking about moving back up north. Maybe Baltimore, St. Louis, or Atlanta.

"Most people are moving down here to be safe, and you're moving to war zones. Not that Florida doesn't have its share of sickos . . . but you're walking right into the fire."

"I'm tired of watching from a distance. You have to put fires out before they burn everything down. Somebody's got to do it. People need help," she said with the conviction of a zealot. It sounded like Trisha wanted to be a missionary, not in Africa or South America but in the inner city. She wanted to save the souls in the broken communities of the U.S. Watching her continue on her way to the dog park, I had to admire the little firebrand.

They haven't moved yet, so I'm thinking maybe the husband put his foot down. But Trisha is a determined woman, so we'll have to wait and see what happens.

THE GUY I NEVER MET

Just down the road, on the way to the main gate, there was furniture on the street at lot number seventy-three. It struck me as strange because months earlier, the house was being worked on. I'd wave when I passed the guy working at his table saw in the driveway. He wore a New York Yankees ball cap, which matched the license plate on the escalade parked in front. A spry fellow, early sixties, salt and pepper hair, friendly enough, always waved when people passed. Looked like he painted inside and out, put in new trim and laminate floors, added new appliances, and soon after the moving truck was unloading in front of the house. I didn't see him too much after that, maybe walking to his car or at the gate. I figured I'd run into him some time at the clubhouse or an event at the pool. I never did.

Posted on the bulletin board by the mailboxes was a notice:

The Seaside community mourns the loss of Mr. Gerald R Thompson, Lot #73, who passed away in his sleep on Monday. Though a new resident, Mr. Thompson will be missed.

For further information, please call the office at 772-345-6611

Claire Nobel,
Manager

THE DRUG DEALER

Here's one for Malcolm. A bit of crime and the drama that goes along with it. Although I never had met the alleged drug dealer, I saw how the property where he lived began to be run down. While on my morning ride, I stopped to talk with Ruby, my hair cutter. Three guys from the house across the street burst out of the door and piled into a car. The homeowner, bare-chested with a big gut covering his waistline wearing Bermuda shorts, smiled and waved to us before closing the door. Ruby turned to me and, with a lowered voice, saying, "The guy is selling drugs."

"How do you know?" I whispered back.

"Didn't you see what just happened?"

"Yeah, it does look suspicious."

"I'll tell you all about it next time you're in my chair."

I took notice of the house when I passed it on my morning rides. Drab brown drapes, sagging in places, covered the windows. I couldn't help but speculate about what went on inside, beyond that sad facade. I became curious and went to Ruby for a haircut, even though I didn't need one. She would know what's going on.

I went to the barbershop mid-morning. It was very busy. The barber chairs were full, and Ruby had two people waiting at her station. Grabbing a travel magazine, I sat down and checked my phone. I had traveled halfway around the world in the magazines before Ruby finally came to me. She smiled as she clamped the apron around my neck.

"I know why you're here."

"You do?"

"You wanna' know all about the drug dealer across the street from my house, don't ya?"

"I guess I do. . . . Like how the hell did he even get into Seaside anyway? He only looks about forty-five."

"His mother. He inherited the place from his mother. Poor thing, she had enough trouble with her sickness without having a drug-addicted son. He was no help to her, I can tell you. She had to go to all her doctor appointments on her own. I'd pick up her meds sometimes and bring her some groceries. She was a nice lady. The old girl passed away last year in a hospice."

Ruby was thin, around five foot eight, with long red hair with streaks of silver running through it. Her skin revealed how much time she had spent at the beach throughout her life. She moved down from the Jersey Shore in the nineties and lived in Ft. Lauderdale and Hollywood before settling in Vero Beach. She was very proud of her son whose pictures she displayed on her mirror. A framed picture of him in his Marine Corps uniform was on the counter, surrounded by various hair products.

"Lincoln came by a couple of times to try to get him to move out after his mother died. One time with the sheriff . . . but with no luck. I myself have seen the police there a couple of times. He must have some kind of rights or something." She spun the chair, took a snip, spun it again, and took a cut. "One time, I was weeding the flower beds, and I heard him tell one of his customers, 'Don't worry, they're old. They won't notice a thing'. Whatever that was about can't be good. I've got my eyes open, my ears up, a nine-millimeter on my nightstand, and a dog that barks at anything that moves."

The next time I passed, the metal cover was off the HVAC, and a rusty window unit was set in a side window, propped up by a 2x4. A shutter hung diagonally suspended by a single screw. On the other side of the house, a power cord ran to the neighbor's house. He was obviously pilfering electricity.

Another month passed, and I was ready for a haircut. I sat down, and before Ruby had me covered up, she was telling me she's going to Japan. Her son had been stationed there for the last year, and he met a girl. They were going to be married. A traditional Japanese wedding.

"I'm so excited. I've been watching movies on Netflix and learning all I can about the culture. There's even an opera about a Japanese wedding. You like operas, don't yah?"

"Yeah, sure, you're talking about Madam Butterfly."

"That's it, Madam Butterfly. What a pretty name."

"That's wonderful! When are you leaving?"

"In six months. They sign some kind of contract, wait awhile, and then get married later."

"Congratulations, Ruby, your family has become international. All the best. . . . So, what else is new? What's happening with your friend across the street?"

"He has no central air anymore, just some old window unit. How does he live in there?" she said, staring at me through the mirror. "It must be full of mold."

"I guess so?"

"I don't think he's paying his lot rent either cause they nailed some papers on his door. And listen to this. There has been a string of robberies lately in Seaside, and guess what?" I shrugged my shoulders. "All the break-ins happened along the road from the front gate to his house. How's that for dumb?"

"They must be on drugs." We laughed loudly, attracting the attention of all the chairs in the row. "Nobody saw anything?' I said, slipping down. "The neighbors didn't notice?"

"They break in during the night when everyone's asleep. So, . . . they pick up their poison and on their way out they pick up something else . . . or, maybe he's the head of a robbery ring and tells them which places to hit. Whatever, it's shit stupid. The string of robberies leads right to his door. There are cameras at the front gate, and they can see everyone who's coming and going."

"Besides, the snowbirds don't leave anything of value over the summer. Not just because of break-ins — the hurricanes as well. What could they get? A TV, an old computer, a microwave?"

"I guess so. That's why I don't buy that kind of stuff at flea markets. It's probably stolen."

"I never thought of that."

"Spread the word!"

A couple of weeks later, on my ride, I saw Ruby talking with her neighbors in front of her house. There was a fire dept ambulance, lights flashing--doors open, in front of the drug dealer's place. The police were questioning the suspect on the lawn, and the place was busy with tech people coming and going. A gurney with a covered body on it was rolled out of the doorway. Long brown hair fell over the gurney's edge, and a woman's shoe hit the ground as they loaded her into the ambulance. We stared at each other without saying a word and watched the ambulance zip away with lights flashing. I nodded goodbye to everyone and rode on, sad and repulsed.

After that, I took an alternative route through the park, not wanting to ride into the bad energy that permeated from the house onto the street. A ride past would darken what was a sunny morning. It would destroy my intention of clearing my head with a journey through aberrant rooms and corridors. Not my choice. I kept to my alternative route for months when I got a text from Ruby. *"Come by the house this morning. There's something I think you might want to see."*

I rode over to find Ruby with her neighbors across the street from the drug dealer's house. A back-hoe was warming up and a dump truck was at the ready. They said good morning with a big smile, and I returned the same.

"It'll take two days, the foreman told us," Ruby said. "After that, it'll all just be a bad memory."

We watched them collapse the roof and fold the walls into a pile. The brown drapes dangled from the backhoe's shovel. The dump trucks backed up, and the slain, dismembered demon was on its way to its graveyard. Lincoln dropped by and said that work on a new house would begin after the demo was finished and the ground leveled.

I changed my morning bike route back and watched the workers level the ground, set the house and install the plumbing and electricity. By the end of the month, the **For Sale** banners were waving happily, and people were stopping to take a look. Lincoln received a lot of praise for protecting the community, and the esteem of the residents grew for him and his performance as manager. When he was transferred to a larger community with a golf course, the residents threw a party at the clubhouse to wish him well in his new job. He would be missed, but they were happy for him. He was replaced with a bright, attractive young woman who would come to leave her own mark on Seaside. The Shire returned to its mostly tranquil, capricious self.

PASSERSBY 4

It's a rainy morning. A typical Florida day, where there will be torrential rain for fifteen minutes, with a half-hour respite before beginning again. In between the downpours, folks leave their houses to walk their dogs or cycle about, scurrying in their golf carts to get to the clubhouse before the next rain. This morning, the coffee is rich, and the Cheese Danish is stuffed to the point of oozing out its rich filling, causing me to lick my fingers at its ambrosia. Today, the morning news on my phone is all hearsay and gossip, so I focus on the world beyond the hood of my jeep. The rabbits and squirrels have reoccupied the lawns, and the birds are bathing in the puddles on the road. Two elderly gentlemen stroll by, leisurely walking their dogs. I've seen these well-spoken gentlemen before; they live down the road from me. One fellow flies a Canadian flag from his porch, and the other, his next-door neighbor, flies an American and POW flag from the flagpole on the front lawn. I've seen them for a couple of years now and I'd swear they are shrinking. They both walk Yorkies.

"The media's talking a lot about an 'Odor of Mendacity.' That's a strange way to describe court proceedings," the Canadian said.

"Stinks to hell and the high heavens."

"An Odor of Mendacity," he says in his Canadian accent. "That line is from '*Cat on a Hot Tin Roof.*' I'll never forget Burl Ives saying those lines. I've always liked Tenessee Williams."

"They could bootstrap taking a dump into a felony. The KGB used to tell Stalin, 'Show me the man, and I'll find you a crime,' which he used to get rid of his opponents. Putin used the judicial system to take hold of Gazprom, the big oil company. It funds his war machine. The guy that used to own it is still in jail."

The dogs relieve themselves on my Northfork Pine and pull the shrinking gentleman down the road.

"We have problems in Canada, too. We have Trudeau, the globalist poster boy."

"Yeah, well, we've got his twin. Greasy Gavin Newsome."

EPILOGUE

Malcolm called from Angkor Wat.

"Cambodia is beautiful this time of year. I'm having brunch in the garden of my forest hotel. . . . and I won't even tell you what's on the menu." It was almost midnight in Florida, and I had drifted off in my easy chair, tea untouched. I was going to turn in, but decided to take the call. I could hear the birds in the background, cawing, whistling, having a boisterous conversation. In my semi-somnolence, the swish of their wings caused me to flinch as I dipped my tea bag, gathering my thoughts.

"Exploring your spiritual side?" I mumbled, lighting a cigarette.

"Naw, I'm searching for an animal. The natives believe it's a supernatural being. Shapeshifter, guardian of the temples. The scientists say, judging from the drawings and local reports, that it might be a newly discovered species. The shamans versus the PhDs. Either way, both work for me. New species are always fun and there hasn't been a supernatural being discovered in ages. If it's a new species, I'll sell it to the science community. If it's a shapeshifting supernatural being guarding the temples, . . . I've got a series on *Unexplained Mysteries*. I'm just filming background scenes and the temples for now, so I'll be ready when they make up their minds. Imagine capturing a shapeshifter in the act! That would really shake things up. From the Vatican to MIT. We can only live in hope."

"That's an old one. I think Zeus was a shapeshifter."

"Zeus, Merlin, the list is long. We should be here about two weeks, and then it's off to Vancouver. How are you doing?"

"Same-old-same-old. Keeping busy."

A couple of weeks earlier I had sent Malcom a folio of stories from the Shire.

"Got your stories," he said to the clanking of dishes. I was now fully awake and could tell that talking about my stories was just a pretense for the call. He just wanted to talk to someone. I know how easy it is to feel lonely in the jungle.

Been there—done that. I was glad to help Malcolm out.

"Oh, really. Interested in any of them?" I listened intensively.

"I liked the Jazz Funeral. That one might make a good short film. Lots of opportunities for the camera, and I loved the one about the old lady and her pretzel with mustard. There used to be a Yiddish bakery on the Lower East Side that served that and I loved sitting at a table on the sidewalk with my big, salty pretzel with mustard, . . . just watching the world go by.

Good times. And I like the one you sent me a while ago. I can see the Queen of the Everglades as an animated short along with the pretzel lady... That might be fun."

"I can see that. Jedidiah, Eunice, and the Pelican are perfect for an animated short."

"I think so too. It would be awhile, though. I have to finish up here, then there's the Vancouver job, but that's good. Gives me time to think about whether it's doable or not. I'll get back to you on that."

"Okay . . . let me know when the time comes." I've heard that before. I lost interest, but he wasn't done talking yet.

"I'm still looking for some wild sex stories from a trailer park. People want to know about the licentious and debouched behavior in your 'colony of trailers.' Sex sells, and people want all the details about what they've imagined."

"Well, like I said. Maybe this ain't the right trailer park."

"Haven't you had a liaison to two since you've been there?"

"A few, but I'm not gonna put that out there for all to see. They're my friends. Their appetites and desires bring a smile to my face. I ain't gonna trash it up."

"Well, what about everyone else? You can't tell me they're all sitting around knitting in front of the TV."

"I don't know! Do you know about the sex life of the people in your building?"

"Of course I do!"

"Wait! There was a notice from the office on the bulletin board," I said, smiling at the thought, "admonishing those residents who attended the midnight, full moon, nude pool party. *These activities do not reflect the values of the community and will not be tolerated.* They threatened the old geezers with jail."

Malcolm was getting excited. "That would be great! Take pictures of it text time."

" I'm not gonna do that. I may never be able to unsee what I saw." The creepy voyeur side of Malcolm was coming out.

"You're a prude."

"I'm not a prude. I'm just not lewd, is all."

"A thunderous disappointment. We could be on to something big. Well, listen, I've got to get inside. The insects here eat everything that's not made of stone. I'll get back to you on the other stuff later. Gotta go. Ciao for now."

"Bye, Malcolm, stay safe."

It was after 1:00 am. I put my tea cup in the sink and went to the comfort of my bed and much-needed sleep. Fluffing the pillow, I lay my head down, thinking, *'Sex in the Shire.' Maybe it could be something big.*

Thank you for Reading The Shire
Please post a review on Amazon.

Other books by Walter E. Ledwith

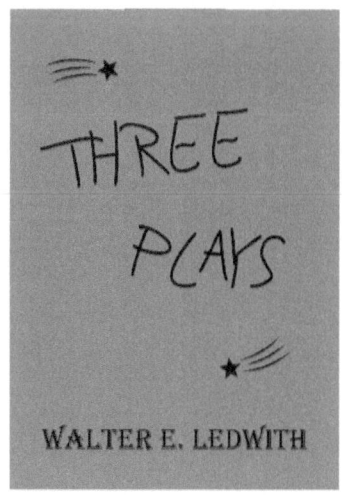